Tower Falls

Oliver Tower

Tower Falls

Cover Design
Brilliant Book Press
Sheryl Hamilton Chaney
Nettie Harris

Published by
Brilliant Book Press
http://www.kristen-bailey.com/bbpress.html

ISBN 978-6151-6320-8

Printed in The United States of America

Table of Contents

Table of Contents

Tower Falls

CHAPTER 1

Shakespeare Festival In New Strafford

Dickie left the theater through the side entrance and started down the stairs, intending to go to the Lucky Clover, his favorite bar away from home. Whispering under his breath, "Whew, got out of there just in time. Annie and Letty Tower nearly caught me. Being nice to them is the last thing on my mind right now." At the bottom of the stairs, he stopped for a moment, letting his eyes adjust. Straightening his collar, he stroked his mustache before turning into the darkness toward the bar.

"Where did this trail come from? How did I get off the beaten path?" he asked himself out loud. Before he could get back on the trail that skirted the park, he heard muffled voices in the distance. Two men were disagreeing violently about something. A scuffle followed, then the voices seemed to be coming his way. Fleeing, he ran for some rhododendrons nearby, but stumbled and fell in the bark mulch that surrounded the shrubbery.

The voices were getting nearer—too near. Dickie rolled himself under some over-hanging limbs and waited for them to pass, and then slowly pulled himself to his feet. The street light was out. He groped his way through the blackness and fell headlong over something in his path. *The two angry voices,* he thought. In a state of panic, he hit the button on

7

his camera causing the flash to go off. The brief second of light showed one man kneeling over another as a flash from a gun illuminated blood splattering on a brightly colored Hawaiian shirt, worn by the man on the ground. The kneeling man slumped and fell. At the same instant, Dickie jumped as a branch scratched him in the ear. He could feel his skin leaving his body looking for a place to hide. His blood ran cold.

"It's about time you showed up," said the man in the Hawaiian shirt. "A minute more and I'm the one who wouldn't be breathing. Help me get him off, he weighs a ton."

Dickie stifled an "Oops," realizing the Hawaiian shirt had mistaken him for someone else. He scrambled to his feet and ran, chased by the darkness. He ran into more bushes and lost his balance again. Down he went, up, he didn't even realize that he'd lost a shoe. He could hear his pursuer, close behind. *The Hawaiian shirt or an unknown pursuer?* He fell again! "Oh no!" He crawled under the bushes and flattened himself as close to the ground as he could. *Katherine's going to kill me! I've got mud all over myself!* He remembered his earlier conversation with Katherine *"I've seen this whole blasted thing twenty times already. I'm outa here!"*

"Dickie, I haven't seen it. Please stay, you promised."

"I don't think I can take 'The Tempest' one more time, especially after dark, anyway, I have a tempest of my own. I'm not in the mood—I'm leaving! I'll take the camera and go take some pictures."

"In the dark?" He thought of her look of disappointment and anger.

"It's okay, Katherine, let him go. You can sit with me. Dickie, your loss is my gain."

"Penn better hope he was joking! Damn him. My wife and my best friend. No, never!" He breathed.

"He's harmless, Baby, Jonah'll keep an eye on him for me. I'll make it up to you later."

"Dickie, are you coming back here?"

"I'll meet you back at our room."

"What time?"

"In time to enjoy the hot tub before bed, love."

The sprinkler was coming his way. He scooted through the

bark mulch in an attempt to elude the antagonizing figure who was too close for comfort. The thick brush covered him completely. Dickie clung to the Rhododendron, hoping his breathing wouldn't betray him. The figure poked and kicked at the brush for a few minutes and then disappeared.

"It's clear!" he whispered. He leapt to his feet, then ran, surprising himself with his speed and surge of adrenaline. *Not bad for an over-easy hippie.* He struggled to catch his breath.

Once safely under a street light, he stopped and leaned against the pole for a moment before he began brushing the mud and leaves off his clothing, and then walked toward the bar, thankful he had eluded whoever that was—*the bad man. I wonder if the other man is still alive? Good Lord in heaven! I took a picture of that! What if it was a real murder? That man looking for me would be the murderer—and I have a picture of him. Maybe I should go to the police—no, I can't do that. I have blood on me! The police would think I killed him! I'm a college professor, I can't get mixed up in anything like this.*

He stumbled in through the door to a din of loud music and the smell of stale beer. In a state of incoherency, he tried to explain to the bartender what had transpired in the park. Acting as if he had heard this story dozens of times before, the bartender, a fat, bald man who laughed too loud, sat Dickie's sunrise in front of him. Other people were pouring in, but Dickie was afraid to turn and look. *What if the killer follows me in here? What if he can recognize me? Will I be able to recognize him? How much blood is on me? Does it show? Guess not, or no one seems to notice. Maybe there is no blood and I'm just losing it.*

"I lost my shoe, maybe the killer's got my shoe." He was suddenly self-conscious of his soggy-socked foot and then the thought struck him . . . *maybe the killer's does have my shoe!*

"Dickie, maybe this one'll get you published. Your shoe, that's a good one. Better get it on paper before you forget it. Ha!"

As Dickie pressed his drink to his mouth, he caught bits and pieces of a conversation going on behind him.

"You'll get—money—job's done— "

"First - no go— "

"—Job, then—money—get rid—the body— "

There's a dead man in the rhododendrons—I need to call—no, I can't! Oh no, what am I going to do? He sat still on the stool trying not to be noticed. He could see the big green neon clover going on and off through the front window and again, its reflection in the wall mirror behind the bar. Rows of shining glasses caught the green and reflected it. Blam! Blam! Blam, went a hundred guns in his head flashing green.

Just within earshot now, the conversation behind him was picking up momentum. "Problems?" Came the husky voice of a woman.

"Just an ole drunk. He tripped over us. His camera went off—no problem, I'll take care of it."

"What! You didn't tell me about this!"

"It just happened. Don't worry your pretty noodle about it. I said, I'll take care of it. You don't want that nice auburn hair to turn gray now, do you?"

"Shut-up! This is business! Henri, stick with this character, we can't have anything else going wrong. Where's the goodies?"

"Goonie took them to the motel. He'll meet us here soon."

"What did you say—a dead man?" The bartender was still making fun.

"Oh aaaa, yeah, a dead man in The Tempest—"

"No kiddin buddy, bunches of em—hey, ain't you supposed to be a literary genius? Have you been drinkin someplace else?"

"Maybe so—" Dickie downed his drink and emptied the change in his pocket, slapping it on the counter as he slid off the bar stool and headed for the door. He reached the street and stood for a moment in indecision. Exploring his options, he took an about-right and started back for the motel. The streetlight just outside the bar illuminated his way momentarily but then he entered darkness. For nearly a block the street was dark and he stumbled over a planter-box on the sidewalk. "Ouch! What's that?" He muttered under his breath. Reaching for a parking meter to steady himself, he clung, catching his breath until he heard

10

footsteps behind him. He let go and ran—*I have to reach the motel. The back door—yes, the back door. I can make it.* Out of breath, he reached the door. *Safety,* but as his weight fell against the bar on the door, it met with a dead clunk. *Damn, where's my card?* He lost his balance as he turned to look behind him. Picking himself up, Dickie grappled to retrieve his card. The footsteps grew louder. Shaking uncontrollably, he grabbed the card hiding between two pansies and slipped it into the door. The door opened and he fell through, running to keep his balance. "Katherine! Katherine!" He took the stairs three at a time and ran the length of the hall. Instead of trying to open the door with his card, he pounded vigorously, yelling and pounding. Finally, the door opened.

"Look at your new shirt! What did you do, crawl around in the mud? Where in grief's name did you find mud this time of the year?"

"I think I saw someone murdered tonight," still trying to catch his breath.

"Don't be silly!"

"I mean it. There was a flash, a man fell, he moaned and fell. I crawled around under the bushes dodging sprinklers in the mud."

"Right! How much did you have to drink?"

"I only had one drink—honest. While you three were safe watching The Tempest in the theater, I was literally thrown into a 'tempest'. There was a woman and two guys in the bar, I had to leave. They were after me."

"I can't believe all this, just to get out of a promise—who is she, the lady in the bar? Who did you roll around in the mud with? You go clean up and go to bed. I'm too mad to sleep."

Dickie and Katherine were having breakfast of eggs and hash browns on the patio of the motel. They had barely spoken and nothing was mentioned about the night before. A picture perfect view overlooked an outdoor pool surrounded with cement and planters filled with colorful flowers. There were large Rhododendrons along the back and beyond that a tall wooden fence. Both had been especially careful not to mention the incident of the previous night. Katherine was spreading grape jelly on her toast as Dickie picked up the morning paper. He gasped as a feeling of terror seized him.

11

Katherine squinted over her toast suspiciously.

"What's the matter?" There was a tone of sarcasm in her voice.

All he could do was point. The whole front page was blazoned with a murder that had taken place in the city park the night before. A large picture showed a man slumped face down in the bark mulch.

"Let me see that!" She snatched the paper as Dickie's face became ash white. He sat numb as she began to read.

"A body of a middle-aged man was discovered in the city park. The identity of the man is still unknown."

Another article detailed the theft of the original handwritten manuscript of the "Tempest." When asked by reporters, a police spokesperson said "there was no indication the two incidents were related."

Katherine looked up from the paper, searching her husband's face.

"Now do you believe me?" he asked. "I want to go home."

Home was Tower Falls, a small town sprawling on the valley floor between three mountains like a picture in a frame. The town and its surrounding area looked like a contour map, each area depicting elevation, in this case, the very rich, the rich, and the others— and the students.

Tower Falls College, small in size, but otherwise well known for its academic excellence was the heart beat of the town. Its grounds were spacious, green and sculptured, and sparkled like Emeralds in the early morning mist from the sprinklers. Various shrub animals beckoned a hearty welcome to the multitude of live deer that came down from Deer Mountain for a change of scenery and wandered freely among the campus buildings. A small creek meandered through the manicured expanse, dotted with cobblestone bridges linking the two sides of the campus. At one end, separating the college from the city proper, was a new addition just donated to the college. It was a man-made waterfall, a miniature of Tower Falls after which the town was named. The falls and an accompanying pool surrounded by a cobblestone wall were donated by the Tower sisters, great granddaughters of the town's founder. The sisters, Annie and Letty, though elderly, were both active in civic affairs and a few private blunderings.

Bordering the college to the East was Eastside Country Club with an eighteen-hole golf course. The course showcased ponds and sand traps and maple trees offered shady spots along the way. Shops and dining areas were for paying members only. The clientele was small but elite. Beyond the country club was Duck Lake and the exclusive residential area of Tower Falls.

It was late spring and wild rhododendrons on the surrounding hills were in bloom. The sun had warmed the earth and the promise of a gold-filled copper kettle lay just beneath the colors.

"When did you buy this Letty?"

"I didn't. I thought you bought it. Does this outfit make me look fat?"

"Where did this come from? It is a nice leather sachel, oldish, but still nice, heavy too. What is in it?"

"I have no idea what is in the bag. We brought it home from the motel. That thing has been sitting at the bottom of the stairs for a long time. Does this blouse make me look puffy?" Letty ask Annie through pursed lips.

"Where?"

"Around my tummy."

"Huh? No, no, Letty. Where did you say we got the bag?" She raised her eyebrows, tilted her head and waited. No reply was made.

Letty wandered away chattering to herself "I should have bought the green one, it didn't make me look puffy." She tugged at the front of her new blouse.

Graduation was a big event in Tower Falls every year, but even more so this year because Letty Towers was graduating from Tower Falls College.

This year, a platform had been erected on the spacious lawn. Faculty, along with community dignitaries had taken their seats as Pomp and Circumstance swelled from the

13

orchestra. The crowd rose as the graduating class filed in.

Dr. Richard Bearzall, college president was also the Oceanogrpher and Physics instructor. He was a would-be graying, middle-aged man, nearly six foot tall. Quite proper in his speech, he over-enunciated his words and fancied himself a reincarnation of Shakespeare. He leaned toward Penny O'Coins, and immediately they became involved in a whispered conversation. "Was last night a fruitful night for you? Did you get the necessary funds? Hey, look at that! She's looking at you. Do you see where she's sitting?"

"No, where?" Penny O'Coins furrowed his brow.

He blocked with one hand and pointed with the other.

"Oh, okay. The funds are in the bag."

"You'll have to make her day."

"What do you mean?"

"Smile and wink and then wave at the silly ole gal."

"Shame on you Dickie! And while we're at it, what about the lewd jokes in class directed toward the young sweet things? Rumor has it that you turn real red as you're visually browsing out the lanky legs.

"Shame, shame and more shame on you, Penn! Going after an old dame for her money," he gave his companion a look of contempt and then a grin.

"Hey! They just called your name. I think you're supposed to get up and say something profound and enlightening." Penn was enjoying this exchange as much as Dickie.

Dr. Bearzall rose to the occasion. With an air of importance, a grave look, and raised brows, he began— "Welcome distinguished colleagues, graduates, families and friends of this year's graduates. Welcome to Tower Fall's College Graduation Ceremony. Tonight we honor the efforts of these fine young people. Graduates, this is your night to shine. We, the faculty and staff, desire you nothing but success in your continued endeavors in life."

Professor Penny O'Coins, a math instructor, turned to Jonah Souser, the Philosophy Professor, sitting on the other side of him and in a hushed whisper— "How many times do we have to sit through this same speech? Last year . . . the year before, good grief, I've got it memorized."

"Come on, let up on the guy. He can't reach his bottle

until this shindig's over. We still have the reception, remember?" Souser was poking fun.

"Yeah, so we can smile real nice for all the people and their cameras," he chuckled.

Remembering Bearzall's earlier remark, O'Coins added, "He's got a lot of nerve! Shame on me? What about the sweet things he's bagged?"

"You're both going to wake up dead some morning, probably me right along with you."

"What are you complaining about? Because you never get the girl? Just the old ladies. Well, lay off the booze, old man!"

"Who are you to talk? Forget about it. We're old friends, remember? We're all drunken skirt chasers." Jonah Souser could have been a college football star—all six foot, six inches of him. Instead, a good book was his cup of tea—or more correctly, his bottle of booze. His slow easygoing manner caught many students off guard. He was a very thorough instructor and his tests were comprehensive. Though graying now, he was still attractive, however, he typified the old saying, "He's so full of head knowledge he's no earthly good."

They both nodded simultaneously in agreement and laughed as the disagreement was forgotten and turned their attention back to the ceremony. Dr. Bearzall handed the podium over to the Dean of the History Department, who would be handing out the graduation certificates.

Letty was last in line to receive her diploma. The lighting set off the sparkle in her eyes and the pink tint in her silvery hair. She reached for her diploma as if a well of excitement was about to spring forth. She stopped mid-stage to open it and broke into an oversized smile as she stood surveying the audience. "Oh, look, Professor O'Coins, it's signed this time, after 25 years." She walked off stage mimicking a very decrepit old lady using a cane. This was supposed to be a private joke, but the whole school knew about Letty's dilemma over her inability to understand math. It had taken her an extra two years to graduate because of this. The audience roared with laughter and the other graduates cheered her on.

The graduates filed out first, then the teachers and then

the audience, all headed for the bridge leading to the school falls, refreshments and pictures.

Off to one side, two young ladies sat waiting for the crowd to thin. "Look at that walk!" The blond whispered to her friend. "He struts just like a Bantam Rooster: the back straight, shoulder squared, arrogant gait, look at that! He counts his conquests as he strolls through the crowd!"

"And you just love it, don't you Angela?"

"It's a long and drawn out, complicated thing. For a short answer, I perform absolute admiration for Professor O'Coins."

"What are you talking about?"

"Let's just say, it serves my needs."

"Whatever you say—you're not making a bit of sense."

"Grandad holds the purse-strings, dummy. There's no way I can make the honor roll. That's his rule— if I want him to pay my tuition, I have to make the honor roll."

"But your name's always on the honor roll!"

"Exactly, I know the right teachers. That's why I called you dummy."

"Oh, I get it now. Angela, that's wicked."

"I've only one more year, then, no more rules from Grandpa."

Later, the three friends, Bearzall, O'Coins, and Souser, converged on the Buzzard's Branch. They sat at the very front for an eagle's eye view of the main attraction, a young dancer who went by the name of Classie Acts, or Angela Goldsworth, as she was known at school. She was the granddaughter of Arthur Goldsworth III, Tower Falls bank's president. Mr Goldsworth was opposed to Angela dancing at the Buzzard's Branch and this fact caused a great deal of friction. He was more concerned with her grades and had threatened to disinherit her if she didn't graduate from college.

When the lights went down and the music started, Angela wasn't thinking of her grandfather or school. The crowd cheered and the music got louder, and she commanded her little corner of the world. Thus, the music started and Classie emerged, long legged and lean. You could feel the excitement and the inhabitants of the front table forgot their standing in the community as they got louder, with shouts of— "Take it off Baby. Take it all off!"

Professor Penny O'Coins, a tall, thin man of middle age, still had a full head of hair and didn't really show his age. Of the three friends, O'Coins was the most attractive. Prone to be just a bit mouthy, he gave the impression that he was a real lady's man and those who knew him probably would testify that he was stuck on himself. His confession came as a surprise— "Letty looked nice tonight, don't you think?"

"Don't tell me you're really falling for the old broad? You're supposed to wine and dine her for her money, old man."

"I have to admit, she does come up with some pretty provocative ideas sometimes."

"Hurry, somebody come give this guy a double shot, he's losing it!" joked Souser.

"Hey Sweetie, double shots all around." Bearzall was getting pretty obnoxious as he called to Barbie, the waitress. However, no one at the table seemed to notice when Barbie didn't show. She had already served them more than their share.

Angela, with a black sequined robe on, made an entrance from a side door and melted into the crowd. She looked around for a place to sit, so when O'Coins motioned to her, she meandered in that direction, stopping here and there along the way, soaking up the attention she was receiving. When she reached the front table, she found his lap an acceptable place to sit and leaned to whisper in his ear with her arms wrapped around his neck. Bearzall, in a coarse voice, ventured— "Here, sugar baby, a hundred smackers, come sit on my lap and we'll talk about the first thing that comes up." He was pawing at the front of her robe, trying desperately to stuff the crumpled bill into her bikini top.

"Dickie, old boy, she's with me!"

From somewhere behind them came a disturbance caused by a distinguished looking, older gentleman. The crowd quieted in disbelief as he pushed his way through, grabbing the dancer to her feet. "You're going home now, young lady!" He turned to O'Coins to add, "If I ever see your miserable face again, I'll kill you! You stay away from my

17

granddaughter!"

Angela offered no objection. In a state of humiliation, she left with her grandfather. Within a few minutes, half the crowd had left. She was the live entertainment. With her gone, only the die-hards stayed.

"Tell us Penn, how are you going to outmaneuver her grandfather?" Dickie Bearzall was always full of questions.

"I don't know offhand, but I'll think of something. Maybe I'll just pull a disappearing act for a while."

"It may be that you've met your match, this time. The old man's getting to you, huh?" ventured Jonah Souser. "Update us on the Letty file."

"No hitches there. I don't think she cares what happens to her money. She wants somebody to watch her dance."

"Seriously, does she really think she can dance?"

"Hey Dickie! You watch your tongue. Thirty years ago, she could have gone professional. We're not talking strip tease here. We're talking real dancing. Angela's got the body to strip, Letty can dance. Tell him, Souser!"

"I try not to pay any attention."

"Hey! I enjoy watching her!"

"What are you talking about?" Bearzall was lost.

"Letty dances out on her balcony almost every night for Penn. It's an easy view for the both of us."

"She likes Rachmananov. You know, that long hair stuff? She wouldn't know what to do with country and western."

"She's a loony old lady."

"She's a well-educated looney old lady."

Annie and Letty, both old maids, had lived all their lives on the Tower's Estate, except for the two years Annie spent studying piano abroad and touring in England where she gave a command performance for the royal family. They were raised by their father who was over-protective of Letty because their mother died of a drug overdose soon after she was born. She was always a very special child and excelled in her dancing lessons. With the formal training she received, she did well, even in her later years.

Contrasting Annie's once-auburn hair and tanned

complexion, Letty's lighter complexion, clear and radiant, was framed by soft curls. Both ladies inherited their father's steely azure eyes. They both walked with an air of a finishing school graduate and had retained their youthful figures quite well. They could be seen daily, walking the parameter of Duck Lake and were involved in the local effort for physical fitness.

The lights from Tower's Estate lit up the lake and the whole surrounding area. Tonight, the lights were blazing bright for a reason. Strains of "Rachmananov's Love Theme" were heard from within. The sisters were celebrating Letty's graduation.

"Isn't this exciting, Letty?"

"Yes! It's exciting, alright. The ceremony this evening and the reception after, all the happy people, the smiles, the pictures. I know that I'm supposed to be happy, but you know what? I'm really not, I'm sad. I can hardly remember before there was college in my life. I don't want that part of my life to end, does it really have to?"

"Of course not, you can attend college as long as you want to, remember? All you have to do is pay for the classes."

"And I can take the math class again?"

"Yes. Won't it be fun? You can take it with me and we can study together."

"Yes!" Letty giggled — "Didn't he look nice tonight? Won't he be surprised?"

Annie, in her protective role, allowed Letty her fantasies . . . what could it hurt? *He truly will be surprised. At least I'll be there, I can keep an eye on her.*

"Annie, did you see him tonight?"

"Who, Letty?"

"My love, who else?"

"Yes, I saw him."

"He looked so fine, don't you think? The cap and gown just came alive on him, don't you think?"

"Oh yes, of course." She tried to hide her impatience.

"I like seeing him in his lewd and lascivious blue jeans."

"What ever are you talking about?"

"That's the way he makes me feel when he wears those blue-jeans, lewd and lascivious, you know!"

"Letty, we've talked about this before, there's a difference between daydreams and reality."

The music played into the night. Letty danced around and around as Annie sang. Finally, Annie convinced Letty it was time to go to bed. She tucked the younger sister in and closed her window.

"No, Annie, please leave my window open."

"You might get a chill."

"Please?"

"Alright, but you close it then, okay?"

"Okay." As Letty dropped off, she was thinking, *I should have danced in front of the window. He's sure to have been watching.*

CHAPTER 2

The Mountain Trip

The next morning, bright and early, Letty, still tightly wound, was bursting with a wonderful idea. She bounced out of bed and ran into Annie's room, "Annie, wake up!"

"Um, Letty, not now." Annie half awake, pulled her covers tightly over her head.

"Annie, Annie, I have a great idea." Letty was yanking at the covers and what happened next was a frantic tug-o-war.

"Okay, okay, you win this one little sister. What do you want?" Annie sat up and rubbed the sleep out of her eyes and glanced at the clock, "Good grief Letty, It's only a quarter after six. You should still be sleeping— look, the sun isn't even over the hill yet."

"Everything's ready to go. We can leave right now."

"Leave? Where're we going?"

"On a picnic! Hurry, get dressed." Letty ran to the window throwing it open.

Annie stretched, noticing the gentle breeze filling the curtains. Stifling a yawn, she swung her feet over the edge and then slipped out of bed. "Have you been awake all night thinking up this craziness?" Now standing next to Letty, she reached out and gave her a big bear hug. Letty giggled as she fought free.

"Annie, the legs of your PJ's are too long. You look funny."

21

"I know, the arms are too long too, but they're comfy, I don't get all tangled up in them." Shaking the arms of her PJ's out longer than her finger tips brought more giggles from Letty. "How about, after breakfast, you get Harold to take you into town to pick up what we need for your picnic while I take care of today's needs here. Mrs. Dustvaffor always waits for my list and I can talk to Harold when you get back about the lawn manicure.

Letty was off like a just hatched goose in a new world, while Annie showered and dressed. *A picnic on Tower Mountain does sound like a good idea. Why didn't I think of that? We haven't been up there since last fall. Letty has such a good imagination. She can come up with the most unexpected things, oh, but this will be fun.*

Mrs. Dustoffer was nowhere to be seen as Annie entered the kitchen. No breakfast smells, then she remembered it was Saturday. The hired helps' day off.

Meanwhile, the Professors, O'Coins, and Souser, were just getting up, and living next door to one another it was almost like one family in two houses. "Hey Jonah! Do you have any coffee? I'm out." He opened the kitchen door without knocking, to find Jonah still in undershirt and pj bottoms.

"Who starts with coffee, especially now that school's out for the summer?" Jonah was hanging onto his favorite bottle with one hand and fumbling in the refrigerator with the other. "I seem to be out of orange juice."

"Gotta have my coffee," Penn continued. "Hey, there's Dickie! What's he doing up this early on the first day of summer vacation?"

"Hey you two!" Dickie hollered from outside. He was standing with his back to them, surveying the lake from their perspective. "Breathe the fresh air, freedom, all summer! Come on out here and see the lazy waves lapping at shore's edge. Feel the gentle breeze." With arms thrown open, he continued— "Smell spring in the air. 'Her early leaf's a flower; But only so an hour.' Hey! Life is being reborn. What's the matter with you two guys, lost your best friend? No, I guess not. I am your best friend, aren't I?"

"What gives you the right to be so cheerful this early in the morning?"

"Ten o'clock?"

"Early for us. It's summer, remember? Besides we're out of coffee and orange juice."

"So, what do you have to eat? Kathryn ran me out of the house. Another one of her headaches."

"Headache, huh? Anything to get you outta the house my friend," said Penn with an ever broadening grin. "A headache is her answer to every ill, anyway, what have you done now?"

Ignoring Penn, Dickie, with a frown, inquired, "Have you got any milk?"

"I haven't got much of anything, it looks like I need to go to the store. Let me see. I have a bottle of Hamm's and part of a can of tuna fish, no mayonnaise though. I don't think I have any bread either." He stopped rummaging long enough to tip his bottle.

"Is he talking to us or is he talking to himself again?"

"Is he talking to himself or the ice box?" Penn was itching for some fun. "Why don't we go see what the Buzzard has."

"Penn, Classie won't be there this early."

"I want coffee, not ah . . . too early for anything else. You guys are getting to be a pain." It didn't take a second invitation to see the three friends off to the Buzzard's Branch. As they entered the dimly lit interior of the local establishment, the darkness inside overwhelmed the bright sunlight. They entered through a heavy oak door and groped for their favorite table. Bearzall stumbled against a chair leg.

"Ouch! Who put that chair there?"

"What, drunk already, Dickie? You and Jonah, birds of a feather." Penn was getting attached to his smirk.

"Can the humor, Penn."

As he sat, Jonah said, "Where's Barbie? I need some orange juice."

"Hi guys, I can't serve drinks this early. Would you like something else?"

"I need some orange juice," Jonah stated flatly.

"Ah lady," crooned Penn, "Be my life saver and bring me some fresh java."

"Do you come with the coffee, baby cakes?"

23

"Lay off the lewdness, Dickie, it's too early in the morning for that, besides Barbie doesn't want to have to deal with that, she's a lady."

"Remarks like that shock the buzzard, even," said Barbie, motioning to the opposite wall.

The three turned to examine the stuffed buzzard, perched on a gnarled oak branch on the wall behind them. "He does give this place a touch of atmosphere, albeit dead," stated Jonah as the three eyed the empty lounge.

There was a dance floor and a raised performance area, with curtains all around that opened at the center to expose a high mountain scene on the wall behind. The massive bar off to one side, with it's plush padding, and shinny top was lined with bar stools that matched the bar. The tables and chairs were fashioned after a ship captain's quarters. There were several small porthole windows high on the outside wall.

Soon, the three were deep in discussion over their coffee and orange juice.

"How did Letty ever graduate?" Bearzall was still geared in a school mode.

"Shift into summer vacation, Dickie. Why worry about her now?"

"I was just wondering. Strange."

"What would stop her from graduating, except math?"

"You know what I mean . . . she's so out of it, sometimes."

"Sometimes, is the key word here, don't you think, Jonah?"

"Yes. She's controlled, to a certain degree, by her surroundings. When she's at school, her mind is programmed in that mode."

"Annie graduates next year, doesn't she?"

Jonah looked at Dickie with a frown— "I think so . . ." he gestured nonchalantly.

"Notice how closed mouthed he is about Annie," Penn was obviously amused.

"What is it he doesn't want us to know?" Dickie could see the fun coming.

"I can't say anything, I'm sworn to secrecy." Penn stopped to take a breath and glanced in Jonah's direction. "Of course, if you were to hazard a guess, I hardly could conceal it from you, with me having such a poker face."

"Oh, don't tell me. The both of you? There are rules to protect the students from guys like you, you know!"

"Rules, Dickie ole boy? What about the young lassie that you insisted, 'Must be eighteen, if she's a day'?"

"Well . . . at least she had legs . . . man, did she ever have legs! If you're going to break the rules, make it worth it."

"Maybe they ARE worth it!" That was Souser.

"They are WORTH it!"

"Leave it to Penn to see the dollar signs. By the way, how'd you ever get a name like Penn, anyway?"

"Promise you won't laugh?"

"No—"

"Come on, Penn, fess up," ventured Dickie.

"I have six older brothers. Before I was born, my dad told Mom, "I don't care what you have this time— boy, girl, or puppy dog, we're going to name it Penny. Anyway, I got named Penny, but Mom always called me Patrick."

"So your name's Penny Patrick?"

"Yeah, what about you Jonah?"

"Ha, ha, it's a wonder they didn't call you P.P."

"Knock it off! Come on Jonah, how'd you get your name?

"Hey guys, you didn't ask me how I got my name?"

"Maybe we'd better steer clear of that one. Ha ha ha."

"Wait a minute, my mother called me Richard. It was my brother who started the Dickie bit. I think he was jealous. What about you Jonah? Did your mother get swallowed by a whale? Oh no, I've got a better one than that! Jonah was the bull-headed one who wouldn't listen to anyone. He got et by a whale for his obstinace."

"Dickie, your Biblical knowledge is impressive. Where did that come from?"

"Must have been from my childhood. Actually, I think Jonah's simply in the drink in more ways than one. Come on, Jonah, fess up. I guessed right, huh—"

"Noooo— my Dad's the one that named me, he said that Mom got as big as a whale."

"This calls for another round. Barbie, another round please." For being sober, Dickie was in high spirits.

25

"I've had enough. The orange juice's getting to me. I have to sit here and smell it. I'm going home."

"Penn, the party pooper, are you sick?" Dickie snorted.

"No, he's missed his matinee. He doesn't want to miss the late show."

"I didn't know you were a TV buff. Hey, wait a minute, it's still early in the afternoon. Not much past lunchtime."

Jonah laughed, then added, "Penn, do you have a TV?"

"Yeah, it's as big as a balcony."

"Jonah, do you know what he's talking about?" Dickie was in over his head.

"Sort of, not quite the same level, though."

"You two need to come with an instruction booklet."

"Here are your refills—two coffees and an OJ." Barbie smiled down at the three.

"Did you season these, darlin?"

"You know better than that Dickie. I can't serve anything stronger until 2:00 P.M. It's the law, remember?"

"I'll see you later, got to go to work." Penn slapped some change on the table.

"Work? Now? Where?"

"Fire watch, summer job, got to keep busy!"

"Letty, hold the door open while I put the groceries in. Even though we had to pick up our own stuff, we're not late for anything. We still have lots of time before dark. It feels good, doesn't it Letty . . . to get out of the house?"

"We get out of the house every day!"

"I mean, you know what I mean. We don't have to go to school for a whole three months. Not really just getting out of the house, but getting out and away, you know? A picnic is a grand idea. Thank you for thinking of it."

"Oh! You're welcome. Isn't this going to be fun?"

"This time of the year is so fantastic, the flowers in bloom, the trees all green and alive, the grass so . . .green."

"Annie!"

"What?"

"The trees are always green."

"Not the evergreens. The others!"

"Oh yes, silly of me. Before I forget . . ."

"Yes Letty?"

"Ummm, I forgot."

Annie soon was in a world of her own as they rode silently for some time. Her mind was wandering back to the last day of school. That special teacher and the messages he sent her way during his lectures had come to an end with the school term. She could still feel the warm sensation that overpowered her when they made eye contact. It hadn't taken her long to realize that he was making eye contact on key words— if she put the words together, they made a message. Excitedly, after each class, she would decipher her notes and add the new message to her journal. The last one . . . *Our last day together, remember this*, still made her heart pound. *Would he ever make the first move? Humm, maybe those were his first moves.*

The long ride up the narrow mountain road was a pleasant one for the two ladies. Up and up they went, spiraling the mountain like a cork screw. The giant trees towered majestically on this warm early afternoon. A slight breeze seemed to push its way down the mountainside just to fill the afternoon with the smell of fir needles. Miles and miles of nothing but trees gave the landscape an unreal look.

"Look at that sign, Letty. 'Game Crossing.' Maybe we'll see some game."

"You look for pawns and I'll watch for the bishop," said Letty.

The old Studebaker came to an abrupt halt near the top. The breeze had stopped and the temperature was reaching an unseasonable high.

"Maybe the trees will soak up some of this heat," said Letty.

"What's up ahead in the road?"

"Drats! Rocks!"

"Rocks? How did they get there?"

"How, indeed! Come on, help me move them," she said as she slid out of the car.

"Annie look, there's Tower Falls down that way. I can even see the lake. Look at the way the sun shines on it . . . it looks like a diamond, doesn't it?"

"Look over there. That's Sparrow Mountain. I see the falls! Right through there, see?"

"Through where?"

"Over there, straight above the Bearzall Estate, see beyond the butte?"

"Oh, I see. The replica on campus doesn't do it justice does it?"

"It is truly beautiful. I had forgotten how high the falls really are."

Annie reached the edge of the embankment with a large rock. "Look how short the trees are. We can look down and see the tops."

"Careful of that first step, it's a doozy. Look up there. Isn't that the look-out?"

"It certainly looks like it."

"Oh, let's go see. Can we? Maybe we can have our picnic up there?"

"Let's have our picnic here and then drive up to the look-out, okay? We can sit here under the tree on these rocks. Isn't this nice?"

"I like it here too. Let's spread the blanket and eat. Look what I bought."

"Beer? Letty, you know we don't drink beer."

"The nice man said it was on sale, so I bought some."

"How could you?"

"It was easy. He checked my ID and I put my money on the counter."

"I don't believe this. Letty, flattery will get a man anywhere with you, I swear."

"Where do you suppose he wants to go? Wait a minute! Don't you pull this Miss Goody Two-shoes with me!"

"Why Letty, what ever do you mean?"

"Remember the man in San Francisco Towers?"

"That was different. That wasn't flattery."

"Well, what was it then?"

"I've told you before, at least a hundred times. I was delivering legal papers for Papa."

"And he flattered you and you fell for it!"

"Letty, if I'd fallen, I'd be dead. He thought I was someone else and when I wouldn't play his way, he hung me by my heels out the twenty-seventh story window. That's not flattery, Letty! That's flattening."

"Do you want some chicken? Here, have a pickle too. Could you pass the chips, please?" They ate the chicken and chips and pickles and Annie even joined in and had a beer. They got a little bit tipsy and giggled a lot. The sun began to tip unnoticed until it was casting shadows.

Annie tried, unsuccessfully, to get the car started, but it simply would not oblige. "I think we're going to have to see if anyone's up there, Matilda won't start. She's acting dead."

"I thought you said you and Matilda were going to do some major bonding before our next trip?"

"I thought we had. Our trip to the theater went exceptionally well, don't you think?"

"Oh yes, especially at the motel, the one with the spa. Maybe Matilda's jealous because we're getting a spa? We'll just have to walk. Oh, look at the beautiful daisies!" Letty stopped to pick one and as she started walking again, "They'll rescue us, they'll rescue us, not. They'll rescue us, they'll-"

"Don't be silly. Oh, look! The tower is just ahead."

"Can we climb all the way to the top? Please Annie! Annie, over there, do you see it? It's huge. I'm scared. Oh my! Its Bigfoot! Run Annie!"

"Letty, don't be ridicules. It's just a charred stump, my feet hurt. Letty, shush! Isn't that Professor O'Coins pickup?"

"Land sakes, yes. Why do I have to shush? What's that? What do I hear?"

"Where?"

"Over there," whispered Letty, pointing. The tall grass swayed with a rhythm as the two ladies approached. Unintelligible sounds rose from the swaying grass. "What's that noise? Are you okay professor? Annie, he's wrestling with a bear, I just know it. We've got to help him!" The grass, nearly hip high, had not yet turned brown and stood straight with gleaming crowns shining.

Two tousled heads appeared as the movement in the grass came to an abrupt halt. "Oh sh—!" Rasped the naked professor as he pushed the head of the pretty blond coed

29

back down out of sight.

"Why, it's Professor O'Coins and Angela. Annie, should we be watching this? Let's leave, quickly, before they see us."

"I think they've already seen us, come on, let's run!"

"Maybe I could just dance for him."

"Oh, good grief, come on!" She grabbed Letty by the arm and away they went down the hill, side-stepping the larger rocks in the gravel.

The two in the grass sat motionless for a moment. "We're in for it now," said the professor. "Those two old ladies are going to kill us both. Come on, we've got to get you out of here. No, I have a better idea. You stay here while I go after them. Maybe I can talk to them. If I didn't have to deal with Annie, Letty would be no problem. Stay in the tower. I'll be back for you."

"Stop Annie! I can't breathe. I have to rest."

The tower and adjoining clump of grass were well out of sight, still, Annie felt uneasy. She didn't trust Penny O'Coins. He couldn't look her straight in the eyes.

"Annie, what they're doing, teachers and students shouldn't be doing, huh?"

"No Letty, what they're doing, nobody should be doing if they have to hide it in the bushes. Unless, perhaps, they're after a passing grade when they haven't earned it."

"On a mountain top yet, so romantic in a way. When Penn is with me, there's always soft music and candle lit dinners." They had started again, walking this time. "Here we are, I'm so glad. This heat is going to be the death of us yet. Oh, my aching feet."

"Doesn't your mind ever run down?"

"What is that black thing over there? Do you think we'll see a bear before we get out of the woods?"

"No. That's the same charred stump."

"I thought her hair looked like that because she was a witch. You know, the straw part. I wonder where she keeps the broom handle when she's not riding it?"

"Letty, I don't believe you, if I didn't know better."

"If you didn't know better, what?"

"Jealousy rears its ugly green head!"

"The grass in her hair was green, I'll have to admit."

"What I mean is that if I didn't know better I would think that you're jealous."

"He said he loved me. Why would he be with her?"

"Letty, come back to reality. After what we just saw, his reason should be obvious. Here's Matilda. Guess what? We're not broke down. I forgot, when I turn the key on I have to step on the starter too."

"But we quit running."

"We stalled. Let's get out of here and go home and look at our new hot tub."

"But it's still in the box!" Letty opened the car door, and then, with a frown, paused, looking over the top of the car, she asked, "Do you want me to help you drive?"

"You can be the back seat driver, okay?"

"I can do that. How exciting!" She closed the front passenger door and opened the back door on the passenger side and climbed in. "Annie, where is the steering wheel?"

"Use your imagination."

"Oh, okay." The bushes, trees and flowers whizzed by as Annie slid back and forth over the gravel road. Letty, driving from the back, ventures, "What are you doing? Slow down, watch out for that rock."

"Pipe down," came Annie's retort. "I'm concentrating on where I'm going."

All was quiet for quite a while as Letty turned her imaginary steering wheel and helped Annie make the corners then, "Oh no! Oh Annie, I've done it! Oh dear God, I've done it!"

Annie hit the brakes and slid to a stop, "What's wrong?" She turned to see Letty go white— her eyes, wide with terror.

"I'm sorry Annie. I've killed us both, just like in Driver's Ed. Didn't you see me put us both over the cliff?"

"Letty, what on earth are you talking about?"

"And he'll get all my money!"

"Who? Who's he? Letty, come back to reality and tell me what you're talking about."

As Letty's eyes came back into focus, "Why are we stopping here?"

"Because you- Never mind, let's just go home, then we'll have a nice long talk about what happened." They were both uneasily quiet the rest of the way home. "It's finally beginning to cool some." said Annie as they pulled into the driveway. "I'll put Matilda to bed while you unlock the house. Turn the porch light on too."

The house built by their great-grandfather had remained the same for many years. The ladies were the fourth generation to live in the old house, a land monument in this small community. A glimpse of the grounds with the mansion-like structure surrounded by majestic elms and ash, earned awed reverence from the tourists. It remained the same over the years with few changes and caused quite a stir when Annie ordered a mason to "please come and put in a spa." The whole town began speculating on reasons for the change. Undaunted, the ladies continued with their plans. The solarium was to become a "Planet Venus," a room-full of exotic tropical plants, all draped around and partially concealing an enormous hot tub.

Getting out of the car, Annie ran into a shrub in her haste. "All the way to the top of the mountain and back, only to get attacked by a tree in my own driveway."

Letty awoke with a start, *"I didn't dance tonight, I must do so."* She opened the french doors and stepped out onto her veranda. She took a long deep breath of fresh air. The night air tugged at her short-cropped hair covering her eyes. Annie looked in on her to see if she had gotten into bed yet. She watched in amusement as Letty returned from the veranda and put on her favorite Rachmananov's Love Theme. She dipped, swayed gracefully. She tossed her head slightly and sipped iced tea from an old sculptured sherry glass.

"What are you doing?"

"I'm dancing for him."

"What? okay Letty, who is 'him'?"

"You know, the one who gets everything I have when I die."

32

"No, I don't know who . . . and, furthermore, get out of that window! Have you gone totally loony?"

Pouting, Letty did as Annie said but made an "I'm sorry" sign toward the window as she did so.

"Letty, I think it's time for us to have a heart-to-heart, just like we did when we were girls, do you remember?" There was a long silence— then, "Letty, what are you wearing?"

"Can't you see? Are you blind? I told you, I'm dancing for him." Once again, she moved to the veranda.

Penny O'Coins appeared on the front steps of the old house, but confronted with the brass lion head on the front door, he seemed puzzled. "Forsooth ye ole lion head, what maketh ye roar?"

Letty, seeing the professor from the veranda, leaned out and exclaimed, "Just pull the chain, he says meow!"

Looking up, he proclaimed, "Doth my eyes deceiveth me? What fair maiden is it that haileth me from yon window?"

At that instant, Annie's head appeared over the veranda. She gave Letty a shove back through the French doors.

"Bloweth it outeth your tu-tu!"

He stumbled down the steps and bowed, "Pray thee, fair maiden, might thee kindly present me to the lady of this mansion so fair?"

"I am she. What do you want?"

"We need to talk. May I come in?"

"You drunken fool, go home."

"Annie, let me in this instant!"

At this precise moment, Letty opened the door, still in her long flowing, almost see-through negligee— "Why Professor, how nice to see you again today, won't you come in?"

Placing one foot deliberately in front of the other, he advanced back up the steps with an all out victory smile. Annie yelled at her, "Letty! Shut that door! Don't let him in!"

"Oh, I'm sorry. I can't let you in," exposing even more of herself as she closed the door just as he reached her.

Annie came tearing down the stairs— "Letty, how could you let him in after what we just saw? What are you thinking of? Are you having hot flashes again?" She watched with a frown as Letty fanned frantically with her hand.

"Sometimes, you are so dense! It only happens when I get

that close to him."

"Oh for Pete's sake, you're twenty years older than he. My heavens, have you lost your senses?"

"I knew you would make fun of me. That's why I never told you."

"Are those real tears? Letty, I'm sorry. I didn't mean to make you cry. Forgive me?"

"Yes, I forgive you, anyway you're my sissy. Let's go look at our new hot tub."

"But it's only a hole in the ground."

"I know, but I like to look."

"Okay, lets fantasize. Did you remember to lock the front door?"

"It's not my turn."

Another voice interrupted them.

"It's not nice to turn your backs on a guest." That was Penny O'Coins.

"Letty! You didn't lock the door behind you! Get out of here, you drunken fool! Out!"

"Not until we talk about this afternoon. You were on the hill this afternoon, I saw you, the both of you. I know you were there. I'm not leaving until you listen. She came up there and was all over me. I was trying to fight her off." He reached out and took Letty by the arm as if to hold her captive until he got an answer.

"Let go of her this instant!" Annie gave him a push and kicked at him at the same time. He lost his hold on Letty as he swerved to miss Annie's foot, slipped and went head-long in the hole dug for the hot tub. "Get out of that hole this instant! Letty, call the police."

"Annie, he's not moving. I don't think he heard you."

Annie leaned over the hole, squinting to see, "Do you suppose he's unconscious?"

"I don't know. Look, his head hit that pipe, and there's blood. . . oh Annie."

"Oh no! He can't be dead. I didn't mean him any harm. I just wanted him out of here. I didn't want him to hurt you. We've got to do something."

"He looks . . . kinda, you know, dead! Maybe we'd better call the police."

"No! Let me think. If the hot tub were only installed, we could get in and think this through. That's it! If the hot tub were already installed and he was under it, no one would ever know. Help me bury him. We can't go to prison. It's dark outside now. I'll drive his pickup away and wipe the finger prints off the steering wheel and when they find it, they just won't find the professor."

The two ladies worked laboriously into the night. Annie drove the pickup out to the lake. At the other side, she released the emergency brake, put the truck in neutral and watched it roll into the water and sink slowly out of sight. She stood to watch the bubbles for just a moment— "Please go away, bubbles, no more bubbles, please!" Annie whispered, startling herself. The moon was almost gone, the sky to the East would begin to lighten soon and she had a mile and a half to walk. *I've got to hurry. I've got to get back. Letty will dig him up. I just know she will. I hope she's still polishing the silver when I get back, anything to keep her mind off him.*

Penny O'Coins, his blood, and his pickup were all gone as the sun rose early to greet a new day.

CHAPTER 3

Jonah Souser Gets Et!

Letty went into Annie's room and knelt beside her bed as she tugged on her blankets, "Annie, it's Sunday, you must get up. We need to go to church."

"Letty, I've been up all night. How can I get up and go to church?"

"After last night, we need to go to church."

"Go back to sleep."

"I haven't been asleep, please Annie, we need to go. We need to light a candle."

"You're right. We do need to go. Of course, we'll go. What time is it?"

"Service starts in an hour and a half."

"We'll have to hustle."

It was still early and the morning sun was a welcome guest as the two ladies sat on the sun porch hurriedly eating their breakfast. It was a warm friendly nook, hidden from the road on the back corner of the old house. The smell of sausage and eggs had given way to the fragrant roses near the back corner of the porch.

"Annie, where did he go?"

"He's gone, remember? Dead . . . Do you know what dead means?"

Letty burst out crying. "Remember our kitten Annie?"

"Yes, of course I do."

"Do you remember how she died?"

"I remember taking her with us to the falls. Papa was upset with us so we left her in the car, but she got out somehow and drowned in the pool under the falls."

"Annie . . ." Letty was still crying, "I went back to the car and got her out. She was having so much fun swimming back to me that I kept throwing her back in, until the last time . . . she didn't swim back . . . that's how she got dead. It was my fault the kitten died, just like it was my fault he died." Letty was crying uncontrollably.

"Don't do that." It was hard for Annie to sympathize from her viewpoint. "He's not worth crying over. It wasn't your fault. When was he ever nice to you?"

"He took me to dinner when you were at your photography class, so I wouldn't be alone."

"When?"

"When you were in the darkroom, you weren't the only one having fun."

"Whatever are you talking about?"

"We ate by candlelight and I danced for him, and I gave him what he wanted."

"Letty! You didn't!"

"It's only money."

"I can't believe my own ears! Letty you always have been able to push my buttons. What money are you talking about?"

"My money, big sister. Penn and I went to see Mr. Lyer and I changed my will. Now, part of my money goes to the college and part of it goes to Penn."

"Oh my goodness, I should have guessed. I thought you were giving it all to the college and Father Paul's Home for Deaf Children?"

"They still get seventy percent. Penn has a dream and I want to help him realize his dream."

"And if you outlive him, what then?"

"Then he gets to have his dream in heaven. The college and Father Paul will get it all, after all." At this point, Letty lost it again. "He is gone, isn't he?"

"Yes Letty, he is . . ." Bewildered, Annie was trying to

regain her composure, when-

"Of course, he kissed me too. You know."

Annie rolled her eyes with a resigned look of disgust and amusement, "How very nice! How was it? Was it a French kiss? Does he have false teeth?"

"Annie, you're being mean, and for your information, he kissed me more than once."

"Oh, you made out?"

"Well, that's none of your business, and furthermore, it's none of your business how far we made 'out'." She accentuated the "out" with fingers and a smirk of satisfaction.

"Come on, tell me how far."

"Well, far enough to know he wears underwear with dollar signs on them, so there!"

"Letty, you didn't!"

"I know he has a wee willy," she added smugly with a flowing hand gesture.

"A what?"

"You know," waving her hand with a superior air that comes from experience.

"Oh fine, you had an affair. You should be proud of yourself. You and your 'Wee Willy'!"

"You're angry," she said, tearfully, "Or maybe you're jealous. That's it! You're jealous!"

"Letty, is this another one of your day dreams?"

"Annie, you don't believe me, do you?"

"Well-"

"I know, I can show you the locket he gave me. It's 14k gold, see? I wear it all the time. See? Here it is, I told you. When you're in love, you're always young. He told me he would love me always. He gave me this locket as a symbol of our youth and our love, and that's why I keep getting younger."

"Oh posh, finish your tea!" Annie paused to regroup, "Letty, we can't talk about this anymore, besides, we'll be late for church."

Letty was unusually quiet as they rode toward town.

"The men will be coming tomorrow to install our new hot tub, isn't that nice? We will be on our best behavior while

39

they're here and after they leave, we can try out our very own hot tub, okay?"

"Annie, are they going to put the rubies in just like I want them?"

"Yes, 'M's' all around the sides and two big ones on the bottom."

"Marilyn would like that, yes she would. Annie, when the men are through, can we fill it and get in?"

"I think so. We'll ask them to fill it for us, okay?"

"Harold, I found this old satchel under the staircase. Vere did it come from?" the sisters' housekeeper asked.

"Lemme look, Ulga. This might be what was stolen down at Strafford. Naw, Miss Annie or Miss Letty wouldn't steal anything." The grounds' keeper took the satchel.

"No!" Ulga was wringing her hands.

"Don't ya worry yourself none. I'll take care of it." He gave Ulga a quick smile and a wink.

Letty slipped into a confessional booth and knocked. "Father Paul, are you there?"

"Yes, my child, I'm here. Do you have a confession to make?"

"I think so. Well, sort of. Yes, I guess I do, but how do I begin?"

"What did you do wrong, my child? Just start from the beginning."

"She kicked him into the hole and the truck drowned and we buried him, and I polished all the silver."

Clearing his throat, Father Paul thought to himself, *I'm missing something here.* He spoke softly as he said, "God forgives us if we're truly repentant my child, say three Hail Mary's, light a candle and go in peace." *Do I really want to know what's going on here?*

"Oh, thank you so much, Father. I feel so much better now." Letty returned to her seat beside Annie in the pew, all smiles. "I feel so much better. Father Paul said we have to light a candle and to go in pieces."

"What? Letty, what have you done?"

"I went into the booth over there and talked to Father Paul, and he said to go in pieces."

"You did what?"

"I told Father Paul everything."

"Letty, I can't believe you would blab to the first person you see."

"It's okay. He said God forgives us. We must light a candle, say three Hail Mary's and go in pieces. Isn't that nice?"

"I think Father Paul said 'peace' not pieces."

"Yes of course he did, how foolish of me!"

"Letty, aren't you forgetting something?"

"What am I forgetting?"

"We're not Catholic."

"Oh, I forgot."

Annie left Letty sitting in the pew and walked toward the front where Charity Townsend and her family were standing. Charity, a secretary for the college, saw her coming— "Annie, how nice to see you here. I haven't seen you in church before, have I."

"No. Letty talked me into it this morning. I'm so glad I came now. Perhaps we'll come more often." Pulling her aside, Annie asked, "Charity, can we talk for a minute?"

"Annie, you look pale. Is something wrong?"

"I had a rough night, but that's not what I want to talk to you about. Letty and I weren't brought up Catholic and we know nothing about the church. Are confessions truly between you and the priest?"

"Absolutely! Between you, the priest, and God."

Annie sighed deeply. "Well— that's a relief," leaving Charity wondering what was going on. Perceiving her frown, she continued, "Letty just confessed and I have no idea what she might have confessed."

"I love Letty's stories. She was telling the children a story about her great grandfather and his Indian Princess last week. I've never heard that one before."

"That story is actually based on a truth. Our great grandfather did marry the daughter of an Indian chief. She was supposed to have been very beautiful. One of his journal entries related, 'God has created only one utopia and I have found it for my beautiful princess.' He was talking about Tower Falls. She wasn't as homesick for her people when she sat near the falls, so he built her a mansion in the valley below. They journeyed up the mountain to the falls often. His journal is full of descriptions of this area and he was so elegant with words. I love to read it. I've even considered trying to publish it."

"I think that's a wonderful idea. A part of our town's history."

"And the proceeds could go to Father Paul's School. I'm liking the whole idea more and more. Charity, would you like to read the journal and tell me what you think?"

"I'd love to."

Out through the old solarium window, now remolded, were numerous flowers: peonies, pansies, blue bells and lilies. Rhododendrons lined the far side of the yard, partially hidden by large elm and hickory trees and the expansive lawn sprawled, giving it a look of an old Southern estate. The thick wall around the perimeter was beginning to decay and the gate in front was altogether non-existent now. Ivy hid much of the ironwork which otherwise would have stood rusted with age. It was through this gate that Jonah Souser, very inebriated, entered, looking for his friend Penny O'Coins. The two of them had been drinking together days earlier and O'Coins confided that he was interested in Letty's handsome estate. He wandered the grounds until finally he found his way into the remodeled parlor and fell head long into a humongous man-eating plant. The minute his head hit her sensuous lips, she enveloped it within her grasp. The old ladies, christening their new hot tub, heard muffled cries and then something that sounded much like a succulent, passionate sound.

"Letty, did you remember to feed Jezebel?"

"It wasn't my turn!"

"It was too!"

"No, it wasn't, it was my turn yesterday."

The muffled cries ceased and the ladies promptly forgot about them.

A few minutes later, Charity appeared, "Hello, is anyone

here?"

"We're in here, dear, who is it?"

"It's Charity. I knocked but no one heard, the door was open. I brought your journal back. This is absolutely great, Annie, I love it - Oh my goodness, help! Poor Mr. Souser! How did this happen? What is this? Someone . . . help!"

"It wasn't my turn, Annie."

"Professor, oh my goodness! Charity, I'm so sorry for all this. Help me pull him away from Jezebel. Let's get this poor man away from Jezebel." The two worked laboriously pulling Jonah Souser free. "Professor Souser, can you hear me? Oh my goodness." Annie bent down over the professor, lifting his head and cradling it in her arms, she looked back over her shoulder, "Letty, go get some fresh meat."

Letty returned with a raw chicken leg.

"Here you are, my precious. That's a good girl. Tomorrow mama will give you the breast."

"Shouldn't someone call a doctor?" Charity asked.

"We have a medicine plant. His name is Rappacinni . . . but let's try some whiskey first. That'll fix him up quick enough. That's what they do in the movies," Letty stated flatly.

"My heavens, his face is really red and swollen. I think he needs a doctor. Please call a doctor."

"Whiskey? Letty, we don't have any whiskey."

"I bought it for you-know-who. I'm sure that when he gets some feeling back in his face, he'll be fine."

"We'll discuss this later, just go get it! If this doesn't work, we'll have to call a doctor."

"Why, I'm not ill."

"No Letty, for the professor."

"My professor isn't here."

"For poor Professor Souser, Letty . . . oh dear, Professor, you're all wet!"

"You were the one all over him, not me!"

"Hush your nasty mouth!"

"That's my fault," said Charity. "I thought water would help, so I got that empty glass from over there and filled it with water from the hot tub. I'm afraid all it did for him was get him wet and cold."

43

"I'm cold too," said Letty. "Maybe we should put him in the hot tub."

"Letty, we had a hard enough time just pulling him away from Jezebel. How in the world would we get him clear over there?"

Jonah Souser had been lethargic through all this, but finally began moaning—

"I don't think he can talk. He should be getting some feeling."

He stirred and his eyes came open— wide open. He tried to say something, but it came out jumbled and finally, with a great deal of effort: "Oh my head. That must have been some bender, how the hell did I get here? Is there any way I can find a drink around here?"

"Professor Souser, are you alright?"

"Is that you, Charity? What are you doing here? What am I doing here? Where am I?"

"Returning Annie's journal, and I've been looking for you all morning. You still haven't given me your term grades, they have to be turned in by 3:00 today."

"I forgot! Help me up."

It took all three ladies to help him off the floor.

"See, no worst for the wear. Jezebel just loves you sooooo much!"

"Jezebel?" Steadying his senses, he turned toward the plant. The frown on his face indicated confusion. "Tell me that plant didn't try to eat me. At this point, tell me anything, as long as it makes sense."

"Letty forgot to feed her," confided Annie, about to unravel.

"Might I suggest that you move that plant? Maybe even put up a sign to warn people. Is my face still red?"

"Just a little, you're still a little puffy under the eyes."

"I don't think Jezebel did that," said Letty.

"Charity, I'll meet you back at the office. I have the grades laying on my desk."

Annie and Letty saw the two off. "He certainly has a nice car, doesn't he?" Annie was absent-absentmindedly talking out loud.

"Last one back in the hot tub is a rotten egg."

"Now, tell me about the whiskey."

"What whiskey?"

"You know very well, the stuff you were pouring down the professor's throat that came out of thin air."

"Oh, that! I told you, I bought it for him."

"And I suppose you've let him in the house before?"

"Well, no, but I unlocked the door, and danced for him in front of the window, he could have come in."

"You what? You foolish old woman. Are you completely daffy?"

"But he told me he loved to watch me dance." Uncontrolled tears began to stream down Letty's face and she dunked her head under the bubbles in the hot tub.

"Come on, Letty, it's okay, I'm not mad at you, but you must tell me everything. This is really important. The water is cooling too much. Let's get out and have some tea."

"Is he cooling the water off?"

"No, honey, it just happens."

"With something in it?"

"What? Oh, you mean something in the tea. Like what?"

"Somebody's got to use up the whiskey."

"We could pour it out."

"It cost money. I'll use it just a teensy-weensy bit."

At the office, Professor Souser was hunting frantically through papers on his desk.

"Plants that eat people, what will those two think of next?"

"Professor Souser, your recorder said you were going out to the Tower's Estate, so I followed you, but why did you go out there?"

"I was looking for Penn. He had been telling me all about this scheme of his. He was going to hit the jackpot, he said, it had something to do with Letty. He's been gone for a couple of days now. I'm worried. I guess I had a little too much before I went looking for him. You don't suppose that plant ate Penn, do you?"

"You mean Jezebel?"

"They named a plant? They really named a plant?"

"From what I gather, they've named them all. Let me see, there's Jezebel and Dr. Rappacinni and . . ."

"I suppose there's a Scarlet O'Hara too."

"As a matter of fact, I think there is. She's a beautiful cactus, a summer cactus, I think Annie calls her. There's an Emily who just happens to be a white rose."

"Okay okay, I get the picture! Crazy ole dames!"

"But Professor Souser, I thought you liked Annie."

"Maybe, but after today, I may want to rethink my position on that one."

"Annie's so nice."

"Yes, I know, but her sister is something else and you know they're almost like Siamese twins."

"They're both really nice. I know something you don't know."

"And what might that be?"

"I caught her staring at you. She saw me and turned red as a beet and ran the other way."

"Annie?"

"Yes, that's who we're talking about, aren't we?"

"Imagine, puppy love, at our age. Neither of us with a lick of sense."

"Why Professor Souser!" Charity giggled like a school girl, "Oh, this is so exciting! She didn't sign up for any of your classes next year, did she? I mean you don't have to worry about the teacher student thing— "

Jonah Souser was also capable of turning as red as a beet. "She's already taken everything I teach," he muttered. He had been running his hands over his face intermittently throughout this conversation to check for feeling— "Here they are. I knew they were here. The grades?"

"Oh yes, the grades, are you alright?"

"I'm fine, Charity, just worn to a frazzle. This day has been like a nightmare, unreal! Open that bottom drawer over there in Penn's desk, he keeps a bottle there."

"A bottle? Professor O'Coins has a bottle at school and you know about it? Shame on the both of you." Charity, in her early forty's, was a heavy set lady with a heart bigger than she was. She got along well with everyone. Her soft brown hair surrounded a quick smile and pleasant personality. Her position at Tower Falls College placed her within the heartbeat of everything. The college would simply have stopped without her.

The next day, Annie was sitting by the waterfall absorbed in a book when she heard footsteps approaching—
"Hello Annie."
"Professor Souser, how are you?"
"I'm good, thank you."
I'll just bet you are. "What are you doing here now that school's out?"
"I stopped by the library. I'm doing a little research on my own." He shuffled his feet as if he were hesitant to continue— then, "Annie, would you be interested in working on a project with me this summer?"
"I would enjoy that, Sir."
"Might I suggest you consider calling me Jonah?"
Annie's face flushed— she made eye contact and quickly looked away— "I'd like that very much." *How did I ever allow myself to get in such a predicament? A school-girl crush on my teacher. He must think I'm a nit-wit.*
"I need someone to work with me in the dark room developing pictures. I thought of you. Mr. Prints recommends you highly, he says you work well with other people. I have to admit that I'm not so much interested in how well you work with other people as how well you would work with me. I take a lot of pictures, develop them all and discard most of them. I use very few of the pictures I take. I'm looking for someone with an artistic eye, someone who can spot a good picture. Are you game?"
"Yes." *This is better than chasing him around the classroom in my head. It's apt to get me in a whole lot more trouble though. Maybe he doesn't think I'm a nit-wit.*

On the square next to the café was the "Pearl of Wisdom," where Letty insisted that Penny O'Coins had purchased her love necklace. It was Tower Fall's only fine jewelry store. All the shops on the street were done in Bostonian style except the buildings were separate with cobblestone walkways between.

Next to the jeweler's was the "Hippie Hasbeen Shoppe," dealing mostly in clothing and hippie jewelry. Next to that was "Books n Browse." A book store offering new books oriented to college trade, then back through to a side entrance, a below-street-level shop was a bargain book store where just about anything could be found.

Across the way was a bicycle shop. A row of bicycles lined the street in front of the shop. A large sign overhung a showcased window, written in large letters, it read, "Ye Old Wheel Shop." Remnants of the past still hung on the walls of the small shop. Single wheeled cycles and bicycles built for two brought a smile to the faces of the older generation.

"Tower Drug and Fountain" stood next to the bicycle shop. A fountain soda still cost only a quarter if one knew to ask for sarsaparilla. They sold everything in there from home remedies to old Doc Hurt's prescription medicines and greeting cards. Down and to the west of the Falls was "Blow'n In The Wind," styling salon, offering the latest in hair and nail care products, and all the latest gossip. Two things were lacking in Tower Falls. A dentist and an obstetrician. Although there was a hospital below the college which shared grounds with the college, an obstetrician was called in from Centerview, the county seat of Offawall County.

The police department shared the two converted community center buildings with the fire department The larger of the two housed Tower Falls' two fire engines and a rescue van, with sleeping quarters in the upstairs. The smaller held the offices.

This town is so picture perfect. I wonder why no one has taken any pictures and made a post card of it. Or of him. Annie watched Jonah amble down the sidewalk.

CHAPTER 4

The Detective

Oliver S. Homes, johnny-on-the-spot, was always at the right place at the right time, well, almost always. Oliver was a little apprehensive today as he approached the Tower Mansion. He felt intimidated. *It's just the size of everything, so overwhelming, and that fierce lion head on the front door,* he told himself. He looked around carefully as a good detective would, pulled his pants up a little higher, ran his hand through his hair, and licking his finger, combed his eyebrows, before reaching for the large old fashioned chime.

He rang three or four times and was about to leave when an elderly man walking around the corner of the house nearly ran him over. "May I help you, sir?"

"I'm looking for either of the Miss Towers," said Oliver.

"You mean Miss Annie or Miss Letty. They're both around here someplace, I'm sure the car's here, saw it just a few minutes ago. Let me see if I can find someone." They rounded the corner together and as they approached the parlor door, "Oh, there you are, Miss Letty. This man has come to see you."

"Oh how nice. Do come in. Do you live around here, young man?" she asked while leading him into the new solarium.

"No Ma'am, I live over on Cottage Drive, on the other side

49

of town."

"Very well, I must be getting some lemonade. Be careful of Jezebel, she hasn't been fed yet." With that, she left the room. The elderly man was gone too so Oliver busied himself looking at several of the numerous paintings hanging in the large room. He was sure he had memorized the faces in the paintings and was about to check out the plants when the lady of the house wandered through.

"You must be Miss Annie. I was talking to your sister a few minutes ago. She let me in, then disappeared. Is she, maybe a little bit forgetful?"

"Yes, I am Miss Annie. Nice to meet you. So you've met Letty."

"Yes, she's extremely friendly."

"You have to get used to her peculiar ways. She's very special. Did you know that she's on the honor roll at school?"

"You and your sister are both going to college, aren't you?"

"Yes, Letty graduated this year. Going to school enriched our lives so much. We've made friends with so many nice people and nobody laughs because we're too old to be in school."

"Of course they won't laugh, what you're doing is wonderful, courageous too. By the way, what are you taking."

"We're into Humanities. Meeting new people is an expanding experience. There are so many people to meet, you know. We'll never quit learning."

"That's nice. And where will this lead after college?"

Letty came in with lemonade for two on a large tray, which she placed on a near-by table. Then turning to Annie, "Aren't you going to introduce me to your nice friend? Maybe he'd like some lemonade too. I'll go get another glass."

Annie looked after Letty as she left and then back at the young man with a very apparent frown on her face. "Wait a minute, who are you?"

"I'm sorry. I'm Oliver S. Homes. Detective Oliver S. Homes. I'm investigating the disappearance of Penny O'Coins."

"He's missing? Why, I know him. He was our literature teacher. Oh, how awful!"

Letty reentered with a cup of tea. "Oh, hello. How are you? Annie, you must introduce me to your friend."

"Letty, sit down please." Annie patted the seat next to her. "This nice man is a detective. He says Professor O'Coins is missing."

"He's not missing, he's dead. If he wasn't living such a wild life, he'd still be alive."

"Why, Letty, where . . ." Annie was choking.

"Wait a minute, Miss Letty, what makes you think he's dead?" Oliver could feel the air getting heavy in the large room. He felt Letty was the one with the answers he needed.

"It's the life he leads, just like Marilyn Monroe and James Dean, you know, the wild life bunch? Besides, the spa has a crack in it!"

The look on his face said, this woman is really out of it. Her head has a crack too. "Well, okay, I'm sure that must be sound reasoning." To cover his disappointment, he reached for his lemonade and took a large swallow. Choking, he tried to get a breath of air, but succeeded only in a shudder and pucker, but managed to whisper, "I must be going now!"

"Come back and see us again real soon."

"You ladies have a nice day." Fighting back the tears, Oliver stumbled his way out to his car. "Radio control, please. Bunnie, put on your ears. Can you hear me?"

"Is that you Olie?"

"Yes, Bunnie," gasping for breath.

"You sound all choked up, what's the matter?"

"It's the lemonade. The old ladies and their lemonade. I can't get my breath. I've never drank anything so sour in my life."

"You need some help, Olie. My friend Barbie works out at the Buzzard's Branch. I'll bet she's got something that will fix you up pronto. Wanna meet me there?"

"I gotta check in with the Mad Hatter."

Madclynn Hatter was Chief of Detectives for Tower Falls. Her office was housed in a corner of the old fire department. This was where Oliver S. Homes also had his cubicle, which was just large enough for a small desk and a telephone. Bunnie Mann had another cubicle where she tended the switchboard for the police department.

"Oh, she left you a message. She's on her way to her therapy session. She wants a written report on her desk first

51

thing in the morning. She's taking the day off, something about not getting any sleep all night, I think."

"She hasn't prescribed therapy for my loss of sleep."

"Last one to the Buzzard's Branch is cursed with insomnia forever."

From the Tower Estate, Oliver back-tracked through the city proper and beyond to the town's only restaurant and lounge with live entertainment. Situated in a secluded area rich in lush vegetation, wild rhododendrons and scotch bloom threatened enclosure. On his way, he allowed his mind to wander. He had seen Barbie before, from a distance. She was small and blonde with a flawless complexion and musical voice. It was a good thing it wasn't far—Oliver was beginning to fantasize, wildly. *Oh what a voice—in my mind, your voice flows like honey. It makes the rose buds open— your hair smells like roses—and it's so soft—* She unbuttoned the top button of her top and turned to smile at him over her shoulder. A light from behind her outlined her slender figure as the unbuttoning continued. *She moves so graceful.* "Hey! Watch out mister! Stay on your own side of the road!" The brown sedan behind him was laying on his horn. *Whew! That was a close one.*

As he pulled into the parking lot, Bunnie magically appeared in his rear view mirror—*Now how did she get behind me? I didn't see her a minute ago.*

Bunnie's dark, shoulder length hair bounced as she walked. "Olie, what were you doing? You were all over the road, that lemonade must be pretty powerful."

"Yeah, well, yes." Oliver cleared his throat and turned his head away. *I'm glad she can't read my mind—* "Will Barbie let us in before opening time?"

"I called her, she's expecting us." Bunnie knocked on the large oak door. It wasn't latched and slowly opened under her weight. "Barbie, it's us, are you here?"

"In the kitchen," came a voice, "Come on back."

"Hi, it's so dark in here, how can you see?"

"Give your eyes a minute. You've been out in the bright sun light."

"Barbie Toy, this is my friend Oliver Homes. He's investigating the disappearance of one of our college

52

professors."

"Hi Barbie. I've seen you around several times. We've never formally met though. There's something I have to ask you, but first I want to know if you have a good sense of humor?"

"I think so. I work here, don't I? Ask away."

"Okay, I will. How's Ken?"

"Oh that's cute! Old, but cute, so I'll share something with you I don't ordinarily share with everyone, okay?"

"Sure."

"There is no Ken, not yet, anyway."

Oliver turned slightly pink around the edges which only accentuated his already round face.

"You're a real investigator . . . a detective?" Barbie seemed impressed.

"Or something like that. My boss might tell you otherwise."

"And the missing professor, is this the famous Penny O'Coins? The one who's just a little too old to be acting like a preppie?"

"What do you mean," asked Oliver?

"Oh, perhaps I shouldn't speak out of turn."

Bunnie reached out and squeezed her friend's arm, "It's okay Barbie, leveling with Olie is probably the best thing to do."

"How does O'Coins act," asked Oliver again?

"It's just that, as a respected college professor, it looks really odd for him to be acting so, you know, chasing after a twenty year old. Well, I guess she chases after him too. What a hardship it must be to be chased by all the ladies."

"What do you mean by that?"

"He has quite a following, even Miss Letty's sweet on him."

"So is he a sex symbol or something? I thought the guy was a math teacher."

Bunnie and Barbie gave one another a knowing look— "He's not my type, but a lot of women think so, I guess, and yes, I understand he's a very good math teacher. Just ask all the women who sit in his class. He's that self-assured arrogant type, really charming. Have you ever seen him?"

"No, strange as it may seem. I've never even seen a picture

53

of the man."

"I have a school catalog. I'm sure there's a picture of him in it. I'll go get it, its just in the other room under the counter. Yes here it is, right here, see . . ."

"Thanks, hummmm, not bad! He's still got a full head of hair, that tends to count for something," he said, running his hand through his own slightly thinning crop. "Let's go back to Letty, what makes you think she's interested?"

"Rumor has it, she dances for him."

"What?"

"She is a good dancer. She used to teach dancing lessons here in Tower Falls. Did you know that?"

"No, I didn't."

"And she's famous for her stories of wild elephants and Bengal tigers. When I was taking lessons from Miss Letty, every lesson was spiced with at least one of her colorful stories. Miss Letty and her stories have a special place in my growing up memories."

"Do you ever see her now?"

"Yes, just lately, in here with O'Coins. If there's any doubt about her affection for him, you've only to see the shine on her face when she's with him."

"How does he act toward her?"

"He's interested, she's got money."

"That's cruel," said Bunnie

"But it's the truth, and I don't think she cares. She'll take him any way she can get him. Her money doesn't mean anything to her, anyway. Letty's got the biggest heart. She's a very caring and feeling person."

The Tower's Estate was alive with color this time of year. Pinks and lavenders, blues and brilliant reds, an interesting contrast from the oranges and yellows which would be prevalent later in the summer.

"Annie, come smell this beautiful carnation and this one . . . oh, they all smell so nice. I love the flower garden this time of the year. Annie, look at the beautiful flowers I've picked. I picked them for Penn. Do you think he'll like them?"

54

"Penn? I don't think he cares anymore."

Letty remembered and started crying, "We were going to build a ranch, have horses, and hired hands. The horses were going to be our babies. That was his dream."

"Letty, don't do this, please. There isn't anything we can do to change what has already happened."

Letty's tears changed quickly to impatience. "Some men will do anything to get out of marriage!"

"If he had been a nice man, he wouldn't have fallen into that hole."

"He was nice to me."

Annie, shaking her head as she walked away, spoke more to herself than to anyone else, "God takes care of babies and idiots."

"Annie, did I ever tell you about when he took me to his house?"

Annie stopped and turned back to face her younger sister. "No, Letty, you haven't."

"He let the house keeper go early and we ate by candlelight. He played the piano for me and asked me to dance for him. I must have danced half the night."

"When was this?"

"Oh you know, when you developed pictures with aaa . . . you know who. We drank a whole bottle of Cutty Sark and I still beat you home."

"What, may I ask, is Cutty Sark?"

"Why, whiskey, of course." Letty was dealing quite well with the upper hand in this conversation.

"Forget it. It's our bedtime, I'll tuck you in, okay?"

"Will you sing me a lullaby?"

"Yes dear."

Sometime in the predawn hours, Annie woke with a feeling of terror gripping her. *Oh my, I can't move. What's going on? What in the world?* Annie lay frozen in her bed as she watched a green hue fill her bedroom. The venetian blinds slammed together, rattling loudly. Then she felt herself being lifted, still prone, off the bed, floating out the French doors. Everything was a strange eery glow, yet brilliantly bright.

Then, in an instant, she was back in her bed. Terrified, she fought for control of her senses. Finally steadying enough to stand, *Am I losing my mind or was I just abducted? I need some tea and crackers to calm my tummy.* After a trip downstairs and back, she sat on the edge of her bed sipping her tea, staring at the French doors. "There are no venetian blinds! It was all just a horrible dream. I feel so much better. I'm not losing my sanity!"

The following day, about mid-morning, Annie heard Letty singing as she came into the kitchen. "I'm so glad to see you feeling better." Then she noticed a large grocery bag on the counter. Peeking into the bag, she pulled out several small bags.

"Letty, what is this?"

"Peanuts, can't you read?"

"What are you doing with all these peanuts? How many bags of peanuts do you have here?"

"They were on sale . . . cheaper by the dozen, you know."

"I know you've gone completely daffy now, and what's this, a razor? An electric razor? Letty, what's going on?"

"Ladies do shave their legs."

"We haven't shaved our legs in ten years." Annie walked away shaking her head, "I think you've lost it this time, little sister. Now what are you doing?"

"I'm taking this stuff up to my room. I won't have to wake the whole house when I wake up hungry."

"I am the whole house and you know I don't wake easily."

"Besides, I like having a snack in my room."

"And shaving your legs in your room?"

"Mrs. Dustvaffor, I'm calling from Super Tower's Market. Is Miss Annie there?"

"Ya, wait please. Miss Annie? Telephone! Wait a moment please."

"Hello."

"Miss Annie, this is Reggie Cash, down at the market. It was just brought to my attention that Miss Letty ran up a rather large bill this morning. She bought an electric razor, among other things, and I was wondering if you knew anything about this. We can expect prompt payment, can't we? I mean, she doesn't normally do this and I was just wondering. Well, you know."

"Very soon, Reggie. Thank you so much for calling." *I'm afraid to allow myself to even wonder what's going on now.* She went up the long circular stairway looking for Letty. As she approached her sister's bedroom door, she could hear singing. "You're in a good mood this morning. Would you like to share some of your excitement with me?"

"We should always wake up happy. It's good for our health, Annie, besides, I have something to be happy about. I'm planning a slumber party."

"Who are you inviting to your slumber party?"

"I haven't decided yet. But just as soon as I do, you'll be the first to know. Oh, you'll be invited, of course, and maybe Charity, too?"

"Of course."

"Detective Oliver S. Homes, how nice of you to come back so soon. I'll get some lemonade."

"That's alright, Letty. I'm kind of in a hurry. Hey! What are you doing with a fire in the fire place? It's 75 degrees outside."

"I was burning the evidence," said Letty, with a smile too big to miss.

Oliver rushed to the fireplace and grabbed the poker scattering flaming papers on the hearth. Stomping wildly, he attempted to put out the flames as he shouted, "What evidence, Letty? What are you hiding?"

"Annie and I have to burn the evidence."

"What evidence are you talking about?"

"Why, the evidence that we met Marilyn Monroe, of course. I'll get you some lemonade."

Oliver stooped to inspect the charred remains on the floor. *Uh oh, here we go again!* "Letty, these are just birthday cards."

"Yes, I know. See? 'Happy Birthday, Letty, Love and Hugs,

Marilyn.' She was so sweet. I just couldn't believe what happened."

CHAPTER 5

The Think Tank

"Letty, show the nice detective in," came Annie's voice from Planet Venus. "You must be worn to a frazzle, all the running around you do. You were here yesterday, too. It must be really stressful work you do. Have you found out anything yet?"

"No—not yet. It's still a new case though."

Oliver followed Letty in. "A hot tub is just what you need. We had so much fun while we were on vacation." Oliver handed the burnt birthday cards to Letty, which prompted her to say, "At the motel, we spent much of our time in the hot tub and sending cards."

"You'll probably be seeing a lot of me for a while," Oliver ventured.

"Does that mean we're suspects or that you like our hot tub?"

"At this point, everyone's a suspect, if indeed, there's been a crime committed and I think I'm going to enjoy your hot tub as well."

"Oh good, imagine . . . a murderess. Let me see . . . how did I perform this dreadful deed? Or did I? Perhaps I shot him with my pocket derringer, or perhaps I used a knife," Letty stopped to take a breath, then with a frown, she continued— "But no, this is much too gory for my taste, I think maybe I could just have knocked him in the head, pushed him in a hole, and buried him alive. Young man, you do need to spend some time in our hot tub. It clears your mind and relaxes you. This is where we will be doing our best thinking. You know, if there's anything that needs thinking through, we can head for our hot tub."

"Oh, you mean, like a think tank?"

"Why yes, what a great idea, Mr. Homes, you're a natural. Please join us. You might even find your suspect here." The burnt cards fell in a puddle of water as she stepped in, "Annie, let's make Mr. Homes a member of our 'Think Tank Club' . . . a charter member, along with Penn, of course. Watch out for the crack."

Reaching up toward the detective, Annie whispers, "The only crack here is in the hot tub with me. Won't you please join us?"

"It does look inviting."

"Then you simply must join us," mused Letty.

"It certainly is beautiful. Are those real rubies? What are those, M's all around the sides?"

"Don't they look nice? See the two big ones on the bottom? Marilyn Monroe would be proud, don't you think?"

"Marilyn Monroe, huh?"

"She is simply the most gorgeous woman I have ever seen."

"She's been dead for a long time."

"I know people forget so easily. But I don't forget, I have a very good memory. You didn't believe me about the cards, did you? I saw her, you know. Would you like to hear about it?"

"You saw Marilyn Monroe, in real life?" Oliver was all ears.

"Yes, Papa took us to the set of 'The Misfits.' We saw Marilyn Monroe and Clark Gable . . . oh, let me tell you . . . Marilyn got thrown from her horse and we thought she was dead, but Papa gave her mouth to mouth and she came back to life. He was Marilyn's hero from then on. She used to send us a Christmas card every year, birthday cards too, then she died and Papa died. They died the same year. Do you think that means anything?"

"That's amazing. I really don't know, maybe." Oliver bent

down on one knee, pulling at the cuff of his pant leg— "You ladies go to college, how well do you know Dr. Bearzall and the other two professors, O'Coins and Souser?"

"Quite well, actually."

"Letty's very creative sometimes, Mr. Homes."

"Call me Olie, please. Creative?" There was a thoughtful frown on his face. It really didn't seem to make that much sense to him.

"How can we help you," asked Letty? "Would you like some lemonade?"

"No! Ahhh, no thank you." *Once was enough!* He shuddered as he remembered the first time. "What do you ladies know about Richard Bearzall?"

"Well, we don't know him personally. We've heard stories, too wild to repeat."

"What Annie's talking about are the wild parties." Letty rolled her eyes, "If you really want to know, Dr. Bearzall has a beautiful home and a swimming pool. He throws parties and everyone gets drunk and then Dr. Bearzall supplies the finale. The story goes, he strips, I mean, he takes everything off and jumps in the pool. That pool's heated, you know. According to local rumor, it's the most popular pool in town and you don't even have to pay admission. All you need to do is be an eighteen year old coed with long lanky legs."

Oliver shot Annie a hasty glance, "Creative . . . oh yes. I see, creative."

"Some people go so far as to say that he never wears underwear, so that he can be prepared in season or out of season," Letty continued.

"Now you're gossiping, Letty. That's not like you."

"You're the one that doesn't gossip, I do all the time."

"How much of this can I believe, huh?"

"You do need to keep in mind that this is all hear say. You're hearing local gossip."

"Letty style, right?"

"After you get to know me, Oliver, you'll love me, everyone does."

"Does 'everyone' know when you're telling stories? Hey, I'm not through asking the questions yet. Do you ladies know Jonah Souser?"

"Oh, the tea toter. The one with the tipsy personality." That was Letty, being sarcastic. "He's built like a football player until he moves, then he looks like a wet noodle."

"Do you mean, he's drunk at school?"

"No, I'm sure he isn't," Annie was quick to interject, "You know how stories have a way of getting around."

"Yes, well, you really don't know anything about him then?"

"Why, of course. He's a good teacher. Well liked by all the students. Charity Townsend, the secretary at large, would be better qualified to tell you about all three professors. She knows them better than anyone else."

"Well liked by a certain old lady, anyway." Letty mumbled to herself, but her remark didn't go unnoticed. Annie turned scarlet and that seemed to end the conversation.

"Okay then, that'll have to do for now." He was still wearing the frown. "I just may take you up on the hot tub invite next time, if something doesn't come up pretty quick. It clears your mind and helps you think better? Really?"

"You haven't uncovered anything at all, not anything yet? You don't know anymore about Professor O'Coins's whereabouts," asked Annie?

"Not a thing. We haven't the foggiest notion of what's going on or where he might be."

"This is strange and fascinating," said Letty. "Imagine, us, being involved in foul play."

"We don't even know if it's foul play, yet," replied Oliver. "Maybe the guy just took off for a few days."

"On his way out of town, maybe he stopped to check out the giant man-eating plant and got et, "Letty giggled as if she had swallowed a great big secret.

"Was he here?"

"I left the front door unlocked, but he wouldn't come in."

"I think I will leave that one alone."

The three were standing very near Jezebel. With her shining leaves, she looked very innocent.

"What do you feed this plant, strangers and stray dogs?"

"And tipsy professors," Letty whispered under her breath.

"What did you say?"

"Would you like to be formally introduced?"

"To the plant?"

"Shhhhh. Don't insult Jezebel when you're standing that close. Oliver, meet Jezebel. Jezebel, this nice man is Oliver. Oliver, say 'hello' to Jezebel."

Jokingly, Oliver says, "I hope the fresh meat you feed her is dead first."

"Our nanny ended up dead."

"What?"

"When Annie and I were small Papa usually took us to the Alps every summer, but this one year, Papa decided to go to Africa instead. We weren't very old yet and still had a nanny and a tutor. It was while we were in India that we lost out first nanny. She and the tutor ran off and got married. Papa found another nanny. She was such a nice lady with a sweet voice, but she couldn't run very fast. We happened upon a white Bengal tiger in the bush and were running as fast as we could. Our nanny tripped and went headlong into a humongous man-eating plant, it ate both her and the white tiger and then closed all the way up except for a tiny little crack. We both saw and heard the whole terrible incident. It was the most traumatic experience! Then Papa went to Spain on a boat to get us another nanny. On the way back they encountered a storm. The boat tossed and turned and was finally capsized by the storm. Everyone aboard was eaten by a monster whale, except Papa, who was acting as the first mate, because the first first mate died of something dreadful only a week after they set sail."

"Oliver's a busy man, Letty, we mustn't detain him from his work. I'm sure that he needs to run, don't you, Olie?"

"I really do, yes. I'm sorry about your nannies, Letty."

Annie showed Oliver to the door and on the way, he apologized, "I'm sorry about your nannies, I mean."

"Letty tells colorful stories, doesn't she?"

"Do you mean those stories aren't true?"

"She's always had such a marvelous imagination. You be careful on the road and be sure to come see us again." She stood and watched him leave before closing the door.

Getting out of the hot tub had left her chilled, so she was anxious to get back in.

"That was a nice man. Maybe he needs to exercise more.

63

Did he ever say what he wanted? He liked our rubies, didn't he?"

"Yes, I think he did."

"Next time, he's going to get in the hot tub with us. Land sakes, do you see the crack?"

"We need to call the nice men who put the spa in."

"No! Let me think."

Letty was playing with the bubbles and giggling. "One day in our very own hot tub and already we look like plump puckered plums."

"That's okay, we have all summer to look like anything we want to look like. Enjoy life Letty, it goes too fast." *Why is that crack there? Surely, it won't get any bigger. It can't get any bigger!*

"Annie, maybe we need more exercise, let's join the health club!"

"Whatever for? We walk every morning and that is the best exercise we could get, don't you think? What do they have to offer us that we don't already have?"

"We could do some body-building exercises. They have all the equipment for members. If we join now, we can get three months for the price of one."

"Body-building exercises?"

"Yes."

"Why?"

"You remember, when Penn . . . anyway, you said we had poor old bodies."

"When? Our bodies are just fine."

"Well, actually you said we don't have nice legs."

"What I said was, we don't shave our legs!"

"Same thing!"

"Is not!"

"Is too!"

"Is not!"

"Is, is, is!"

Fine! We have old worn out bodies, and our legs look like skinned chicken legs. Where are you going? Letty, get back in the hot tub with me. That's just great. Go stomping off." Calling after her sister, Annie added, "My, stomping up all those stairs is great body-building exercise, why didn't I think of that?"

Letty hid in her room until dinner and then sat in silence through her meal.

Finally Annie suggested, "Would you like a cup of tea with me little sister?"

"Will you read my tea leaves? No, I have a better idea. Annie, let's have a happy drink and get warm and fuzzy before bedtime."

"Oh, we'll have nightmares all night—"

"Nice warm fuzzy cuddly nightmares. Oh, yes—come on Annie, live dangerously for once in your life."

"I almost let you talk me into climbing the look-out tower. We did run better than half a mile down the mountain trying to get away from the professor. Wasn't that dangerous enough? And what about pushing your true love in a hole? Huh?"

"Let's try for a different kind of dangerous—you know, have you ever needed help finding your own bedroom?"

"No, have you?"

"No—but I have tip-toed up the stairs a few times."

Charity Townsend was next on Oliver's list. "The ladies are right. I should have thought of her before. She works for all three of them. It does stand to reason that she would know more about them than anyone else."

The Townsends lived in a modest home beyond the butte on Rainbow's End. A comfortable house with a white picket fence and a cherry tree in the front yard greeted him as he pulled into their drive. Two youngsters were playing in the sprinkler in the side yard. *That looks inviting.* "Hi, is your mother home?"

"Mom!" The younger of the two, a freckle-faced young lad, came streaking past, on his way through the garage.

"Don't you dare come in here wet, young man! Hello, I didn't see anyone, please excuse my hollering."

"Mrs Townsend, I'm Detective Oliver Homes," extending a hand, "Nice kids . . . I like kids. I'm investigating the disappearance of Penny O'Coins. Would you be willing to talk to me?"

"Please call me Charity, everyone else does. What did you say? Professor O'Coins really has disappeared?"

"Well, we don't know for sure yet. Maybe he just left without saying anything to anyone. Charity, you work with the three professors at school, don't you?"

"Yes," she said with a smile, "I'm what is known as a secretary at large, but I have to admit, those three do keep me running."

"Yes, I'll just bet they do. Do you know anything about O'Coin's personal life, you know, is he seeing anyone special?"

"Well, you know guys, they're always talking about women." Charity frowned. "He has been seeing Miss Letty, but I think that's for fund-raising purposes. She calls him a lot. I have to chuckle at her sometimes. I think she has a crush on him. How will this help to locate Penn?"

"The more I understand O'Coins, the better picture I can perceive as to his whereabouts."

"Oh, okay, I see, if there's any way I can help."

"Of course." At this point, Oliver scratched his head with the eraser end of his pencil. "What does O'Coins have to say about her?"

"You know men. I think the three of them shouldn't be so belittling behind her back. But then, that's the way they talk about all their 'women.'"

"Does O'Coins have other women right now?"

"He has been playing around with the dancer out at the Buzzard's Branch. One of our students, I believe. Angela Goldsworth. Her grandfather owns most of the other half of town."

"What do you mean, most of the other half?"

"You know, the Tower sisters own half the town. Arthur Goldsworth III owns most of the other half."

"Why is the granddaughter of a wealthy man working at the Buzzard's Branch?"

"He is quite wealthy and he's also very tight with his money. He's paying Angela's tuition at college and has threatened to withdraw his financial support if she doesn't make the dean's list. She's a pretty girl and she knows it. She's not much more than a teenager, maybe dancing is her way of rebelling. Perhaps she works those professors the way she works the crowd out there. Have you talked to Dr. Bearzall and Jonah?"

Oliver left Charity's with more questions banging around in his head than ever, *Why would a college professor be interested in a woman twenty years his senior? Why would Angela's grandfather let her work in a bar? Was Charity insinuating that Angela was playing games with the professors?*

"Oh dear, that patrol car behind us has it's lights flashing, Annie, don't you see?"

"Yes, I'm afraid I'm being pulled over. I think perhaps I've been speeding," she said as she pulled off on the next wide spot.

"Miss Annie, you were going 60 mph in a 35 mph zone."

"But officer, Matilda here," Letty said as she patted the dash, "has a mind of her own."

"Are you telling me that Miss Annie wasn't in control of her vehicle?"

"Matilda's part of the family. Sometimes she can be an unruly teenager."

"Miss Annie, may I see your driver's license and registration please?" The officer looked a bit confused and upon inspecting her documents, in disbelief, he asked, "Miss Annie, did you know your registration expired seven months ago?"

Before Annie could say anything, Letty broke in— "It wasn't my turn!"

"I'm sure I mailed that officer, I'm positive I did, because I sent it with the car insurance, house insurance and property tax. I always send all that stuff off together. Come to think of it, I've never received the new tags in the mail. I know I mailed it in, unless . . . Letty?"

"It wasn't my turn, I told you."

"Oh dear, I think perhaps I'd better check and see if my insurance has lapsed too. Thank you so much, officer."

"Miss Annie, your ticket? See you in court."

"Oh no!" Annie didn't know whether to be angry with

herself for speeding, or Letty, for not mailing the bills. *Well, maybe, a little of both.*

"Annie, you shouldn't have to go to court! It was Matilda that was going too fast."

"Letty, are you going to try for your driver's license again?"

"Why yes. Why do you ask?"

"Matilda wouldn't have been speeding if it hadn't been for my foot."

"What does your foot have to do with anything?"

"I wonder if reading the driver's manual will do you any good?"

"I'll just tell the examiner about when Papa was getting his license."

"When Papa was what?"

"When Papa was . . . I'll think of something. He'll like to hear a good story."

CHAPTER 6

Photographs

"Hello, I think I've got this door knocker down pat now. I am Detective Oliver S. Homes. I'm looking for the sisters."

"Ya, they not here. I am Mrs. Dustvaffor, the housekeep."

"Actually, I could talk to you, if that's okay? I'm investigating the disappearance of one of the college professors and frankly, my boss says I've got to come up with something pretty quick or I'm history. Just a couple of questions, okay?"

"Ya."

"Have you noticed anything odd lately?"

"Ya."

"Like, what?"

Mrs. Dustvaffor smiled. "Annie has secret, her man. She has man up in her room. I clean, he stare. I see Miss Annie now," she said as she looked out through the window.

Annie came in and directly put a sack of groceries on the table. "Mrs Dustvaffor, could you call Harold? I have some more things in the car for him to bring in. Hello Oliver. I like your shirt, red certainly is your color." Again turning to Mrs. Dustvaffor, "Did anyone call while I was gone?"

"Ya, plant man vant to know if he can deliver plant you got, or if you go to pick up?"

"I haven't ordered any more plants."

"Then vhat do I say?"

"I'll call them back after while. Letty! Letty!"

"Annie, what's the matter?" Letty asked, coming in from the balcony and walking waltz-like down the wide marble staircase.

"Letty, did you order anything from Sparrow Bush Nursery yesterday?"

"Why yes, as a matter of fact, I did. Passion plants will do well, don't you think? And the lady told me about an exotic plant that she had that was ready to bloom any time now. She gave me a great price on it, I just couldn't pass it up. It'll only cost us three thousand."

Annie choked, trying to get her breath. "What? Three thousand what?"

"Oh dear, Sissy Pooh, you look so white. Are you pulling a Wee Willy on me? Breathe Annie, breathe. Mrs. Dustvaffor, bring Annie a lemonade with a shot of whiskey in it please."

"I'm breathing, I think. Exotic plants, passion flowers . . . Letty, in heaven's name, what are you going to do with a three thousand dollar plant?"

"I'm making a window planter for my part of the balcony. Passion flowers make people passionate. The other one, I forgot the name. If you watch the plant bloom with your lover, you'll be in love forever."

"Letty, we don't have lovers."

"Oh, I forgot."

"Oliver! I'm sorry, I didn't see you standing there. What can I do for you?"

Oliver jumped as though Annie's addressing him had brought him back from a deep reverie, "Oh, nothing at the moment." *Three Thousand dollars for a plant!* "I have to go make my radio check. Maybe I can come back later and join you in the hot tub, if that's alright?"

"Why, yes, Oliver! We would be pleased."

Besides studying the Humanities, Annie was interested in photography. In the elective class she took, the students developed pictures that were usually supplied by the staff. The teachers took advantage of this and brought all their pictures in to the photography class for developing. Professor

Souser was a frequent visitor of the photography lab. Souser was not only an excellent philosophy teacher, he was also an avid amateur photographer. The cash awards he received for some of his efforts helped supplement his teacher's salary. Pictures from other professors found their way through Annie's hand's as well, including pictures of wild department parties.

Annie sat out on the patio off the breakfast nook, enjoying the early morning sun. She often rose earlier than Letty and enjoyed an early morning juice and a chance to be alone with her thoughts. This morning, her mind journey took her back a few weeks to an incident involving her favorite teacher.

"Miss Annie, deliver these pictures to Professor Souser for me, will you?" Mr. Prints smiled as he handed the envelope to Annie.

"Sure! Are these the ones of all the tree tops and clouds?"

"Yes, they are. He's waiting impatiently for them. Some are pretty good."

"Yes, they are."

Walking across campus with the pictures, Annie was thinking of the photographs in her hand. I wonder why he has no cotton candy clouds. As she neared his office door, she could hear him talking with another teacher. She knew that voice. It was Professor O'Coins. They shared an office and it wasn't unusual to hear them passing private jokes. Their delight in this was hard to miss. She paused at the door, but couldn't hear what they were saying. She hesitated, then knocked lightly.

"Yes?"

"Mr. Prints sent me down with your pictures," she said through the door.

Souser opened the door, "Come in. Have you seen these?"

"I helped develop them. They'e nice, but . . . "

"But what?"

"Why don't you have any cotton candy skies?"

"What are cotton candy skies?"

"You don't know what a cotton candy sky is?"

"Apparently not, but, without being too bold, perhaps you

would be willing to show me?"

"They show up best at sunset, if I'm not being too bold."

"Should I leave you two alone? I need some coffee anyway and a smoke would give me some fresh air. Maybe I should go see Dickie?"

"Don't push it Penn," Souser was flushing, "Anyway, that's an oxymoron," Souser retorted, then turned his attention back to Annie. "Sound's like a plan. Pick you up at sunset?"

"Okay," she said, then mumbled to herself, "I would love to get you out in the bushes alone."

"Did you say something else?"

"No, see you at sunset." I'm going to get myself into trouble yet! His eyes are as blue as an early morning sky and that smile, wow! She hugged herself and smiled smugly as she walked up toward the lake. "This will be fun. Oh, I hope we see clouds," maybe one that looks like a desk to chase him around. I must be as loony as Letty, at my age, I can't imagine me acting this way.

Annie could feel the glow all over again remembering the walk home that day.

She stopped by the lake and watched the ducks for a while as she sat on a park bench near the water's edge. That was the day I wrote the poem about the lake with a cotton-candy reflection.

"One of my better poems, I believe." She startled herself by speaking out loud.

"Sissy? Who you talking to?" Letty asked and sat down beside her.

"Myself. Letty is your hair turning pink? Or are my eyes deceiving me?"

"Finally! Someone noticed. He didn't even notice." Letty's eyes were even smiling.

"So that's it. I noticed tons of food coloring at the house, then, poof! It was gone again. Why are you coloring your hair with food coloring?"

"Silly, it washes out and I can have any color I want whenever I want. What do you think of purple for Thursday?"

"What's Thursday?"

"Let me see . . . it is the fifth day of the week."

Annie shook her head, "I had to ask."

"Oh, Sissy, you would look so good in blue, you'd look really great."

I am not going to respond out loud, if I did, I just might wake up in a strange shade of blue.

CHAPTER 7

Detective Gets In

"Are you going to join us today?"

"Don't mind if I do." Oliver made a production out of undoing his tie. The ladies watched spellbound as he stripped before their very eyes.

Letty chimed, "TADAAA!!! I love you in red stripes Oliver, tada-da-da, tada!"

The portly Mr. Homes turned as red as the stripes on his boxers and jiggled as he giggled— "What was that little ditty you were tra la la-ing?"

"The Stripper's Theme," Letty continued with more of the tune while laughing playfully.

Oliver's crimson face beamed. "Do the bubbles come with the hot tub?"

"Oh yes, it comes in a package," said Annie picking up on the subject change. "Did you come to play or are you hot on a trail?"

"I wish it were hot, I'm afraid the trail cooled off. The professor has been gone for almost a week now and I'm beginning to suspect foul play. I'm afraid he might be dead."

"Oh, I hope the same thing hasn't happened to him as happened to Papa's personal secretary."

"And what's that?"

"We went on a vacation to Yellowstone. Papa was dancing with the Indians around Old Faithful, because Old Faithful hadn't blown for a week and they were praying to the gods to restore the geyser to its original magnificent plumage when the earth opened up and took Emma as a sacrifice and Old Faithful was restored that day and hasn't failed since. But you can still see the new crack to this day. Papa was terribly overwrought with guilt, you know, since Emma fell in the crack. He died early too. Did I tell you?"

"No."

"Shortly before his fiftieth birthday."

"What happened to him?"

"It's just so terrible. I don't know if I can relate it to you."

"Oh no, I've upset you. You don't have to tell me."

"Oliver, would you like to stay for dinner?"

"I really can't. My boss will be all over me. I have to check in."

"Oh, but you have to. I polished all the silverware, and the tea pot, and the coffee pot, and the trays, and all before daylight, before Annie got back even."

"I'm sorry, I really have to go."

The two ladies escorted him out and waved him off. Turning to Letty, Annie said, "What were you thinking of? 'Were' you thinking? What are we going to do if he comes back?"

"If he comes back, we'll feed him and throw him in the hot tub."

"Don't joke! We've already done that once."

"Do you suppose he's warm enough? I think about him all the time. I worry about him."

They went into Planet Venus and stood looking into the hot tub. "Look at that crack, it's going to run into the other side if it doesn't stop."

"The crack is coming this way."

"No, it isn't! It's going that way."

"This way!"

"That!"

"Hello, in there. The door was open and no one was answering."

"Oh, Oliver! You changed your mind, I'm so glad."

"I couldn't help hearing you ladies arguing, is there really a crack?"

"I'm afraid so."

"Which way do you think it goes, Oliver?"

Pondering the situation, he squinted this way and that and finally— "It definitely goes this way."

"See, I told you. "

"And it goes that way."

"So there, smarty pants!"

"You're both right, ladies, it looks like a cross, actually."

"Oh yes, a cross, like a burial marker, isn't that nice? When the Indians bury their dead out in the desert, they put a cross in the sand and every time they pass the marker, they add another stone, until there's a whole heap of stones covering the grave with only a small cross sticking up through the rocks."

Here we go again!

"That's so romantic." Letty was playing with her locket. "Annie, don't you think it's romantic?"

"Letty, we really must start supper. I'm glad you changed your mind, Oliver, let's go back into the kitchen, it's cozier." The three went into the kitchen and soon pans were rattling.

"I love cozy little dinners, don't you? Annie, do you want me to get the candles out?"

"No dear, let's just be regular people tonight."

"We're going to have coffee, aren't we?"

They both looked at Oliver and he said, "I'd love some."

"Letty, would you please get the coffee pot?"

"Do you need help, Letty," asked Oliver?

"You could carry the tray."

"Never mind," said Annie, "Oliver, you're our guest. I'll help Letty."

"Annie, can I fix supper? Can I fix my omelet?"

"That would be nice. Oliver, you're in for a treat. Letty's omelets are scrumptious."

"I love omelets. May I help? Annie, why don't you get the coffee pot and leave us two omelet pros to the cooking?"

Oh no! I can't leave her alone with him, or anyone else. What have I gotten myself into?

Oliver waited for Annie to leave the room and turned to

77

Letty, "Why were you polishing the silver during the night?"

"Maybe I was dreaming?"

Oh, fine! More stories!

Annie came back in with the coffee pot and soon the aroma of coffee filled the kitchen. After supper Letty wandered off to her own imagination and left Annie to entertain Oliver. "Would you care for a warm up, your coffee must be cold by now?"

"No thanks, I have to sleep tonight. I'm so sorry about your Papa and his secretary and the nannies, how devastating."

The surprise on Annie's face did not go unnoticed as she stated, "You've been talking to Letty, haven't you?"

"Yes, she told me all about the unfortunate losses the two of you experienced as you were growing up."

"Mr. Homes! Did our nanny get eaten by a man eating plant in India or squished between the toes of a huge bull elephant in Africa? Haven't you heard me tell her 'that's not true Letty'? Haven't you been paying attention?"

"Do you mean to tell me, these stories of hers, never happened? It was a man eating plant in Africa, I think."

"Only in our back yard in a safari tent. I told you before, Papa was very protective of her. She's never been out of the States."

"Okay, Letty likes to tell stories."

"Well, they're real to her, but sometimes it's needful to bring her back to reality."

"And that's what the arguing is about?"

With a smile, Annie answered, "Well, usually."

Oliver found pleasure in his small talk with Annie— "So just how old are you, Miss Annie?"

"Not three score and ten, yet," she answered with a smile. "Old enough to know better perhaps."

"Does this mean you are interested in one of your professors?"

"Where in the world did you hear such a thing? It's no one's business if I have noticed someone, even if it's one of my professors." She tried to act annoyed.

"Come on, you're just dying to tell someone and you know it."

"Maybe someone, but not you." She was smiling, in fun, when Letty walked in—

"Oliver, you're just in time to hear about our safari, the year we went to Egypt."

To the west of Duck Lake wandering with the rise of the hillside was Hobnob Drive. Only the lower end of the road was actually on the lake, from there it meandered with the curvature of the landscape until it melted into the hilly terrain beyond. Oliver had little trouble finding the Bearzall Estate overlooking the lake. *So this is how head honchos live.* He scanned the landscape around Dr. Bearzall's luxurious home. It looked immaculate. Even the shrubbery was trimmed and combed. *Their gardener makes a good living.* The house was of modest size, but everything about it said "expensive." The flowers around the front of the house were arranged in color groups and according to height. A fence to the side was painted pale yellow to match the house. *That must be where the swimming pool is.* After he rang the bell several times, a small, very attractive woman appeared.

"Yes?"

"Hello, I'm Detective Oliver S. Homes. I'm investigating the disappearance of Penny O'Coins. Are you Mrs. Bearzall?"

"Yes."

"Would you be willing to talk with me?"

"I suppose so . . . what do you want to know?"

"How well do you know Professor O'Coins?"

"Well enough to call him Penn. He and my husband are pretty good friends and constituents at school as well."

"Do you know any of his personal friends?"

"You might say, most of his personal friends are our friends too."

"Does he ever mix with the students from school, I mean socially?"

"He's not supposed to do that."

"That's not what I asked. Does he ever?"

"I'm sure he must, sometimes. It's hard to keep all the rules, you know."

"Do you know Miss Letty?"

"She's a character. Everyone at school knows Letty."

"How well does O'Coins know her?"

"I'm not sure how to answer that."

"Has he ever dated her?"

"He didn't make the dates, she did, she pestered him to death. Not only that, he was told to keep the two old ladies happy, they have a lot of money for school funding. Isn't that so, Dear?"

Dr. Bearzall had appeared and was standing behind his wife. "She wouldn't leave him alone," He added. "She spent a lot of time at school. He took her out to dinner not too long ago. We sat together; actually we had a pretty good time . . . Letty can be the life of the party. Her peculiar ways seem to add color to an already overactive imagination. We thoroughly enjoyed the evening."

"Come to think of it," Katherine smiled, "Penn did too. He had a good time. There's something about Letty, she has the ability to make people laugh. Maybe she's not as loony as people think; maybe she knows a good thing when she sees it."

Oliver chose not to pursue that remark or the playful smile behind it. "Do I understand correctly? Was Letty in one of O'Coins classes?"

"Two, actually. She had two classes with Penn."

"At that rate, she'll never graduate."

"She already did and she's signed up for his math class again this fall."

"She graduated and she's still going to school?"

"You don't think graduation will keep her away, do you?"

CHAPTER 8

The Bartender

"Hey Mac!"

"Can't you read? My name's Joe."

"Don't get smart with me. I need some information."

"Go to the information booth."

"Listen Bub!" Oliver grabbed for Joe's collar, but missed, *Oh darn, there goes my tough guy image.*

"Give me one good reason why I should talk to you. I don't know you. I don't even know your name."

"Oh sorry, I'm Detective Oliver S. Homes. I'm investigating the disappearance of a college professor. I guess the sign does say you're Joe."

"That's right, Joe Mixer. I own this place and usually tend bar as well. Good help is hard to find."

"I'm told that Penny O'Coins comes in here quite a bit. Do you know who he is?"

"Sure do, but I haven't seen him in about a week. He was the one Classie was always dancing for. If you can find Classie, you'll find that scoundrel as well. I'd lay odds that they're together."

"Tell me about Classie. Who is she?"

"Her real name is Angela Goldsworth. She's a student during the week and week-ends, her teachers show up out here to learn from her."

"Isn't she too young to be working in here?"

"Normally yes. According to law, she can only work until midnight and then she's only to do her thing and leave. She's not supposed to mix with the crowd. She does though, sometimes. I pretend not to notice as long as it doesn't happen too often. She really brings in the customers. I watch what she's drinking pretty close. Anyway, she didn't show for work last Saturday night. The crowd didn't appreciate that one bit. It was a slow night for me. Everyone left early."

"What about O'Coins? Did he ever bring anyone in with him, you know, one of his friends?"

"Sure, the other two old cronies, you know, the teachers and once he brought in a classy looking old dame and whispered to me, "I'm making her day."

Wait a minute, here, where do I go with this? "Did he seem interested in her?"

"Naw, just her money!"

Okay, I know who he's talking about. "Would you know her if you saw her again?"

The bar was beginning to fill with people and Joe began to fidget— "Hey look, I got pay'n customers here, Buddy, you want information? Buy a drink."

"I don't drink."

"Buy a drink anyway."

"Everything costs money, these days."

Oliver stood at the large door, studying the lion head— "I'll bet you are as tame as a kitten, huh? Why don't you tell me what you know. I'd lay odds that you know everything I need to know." With a frown, he continued, "You don't play fair. Mrs. Dusrvaffor, it's you. Yes. Well, I'm back. Are the sisters here?"

"Na. You here to get in the tub. Ya?"

"Yes, I need time in the think tank."

"Ya? I know something."

"Oh, you have something for me?"

"Ya, I work here tvelve years now, mornings, six days a week. Ya, I think about what you say. Something's not right. Many days before you came, I got to work late. On Sunday, the door was still locked. I go in. I was so happy not to be late to Miss Annie and Miss Letty."

"So?"

"I am forty-five minute late, and they not dressed yet."

"Is this unusual?"

"It not ever happen before. Out there. On the sun deck. Miss Annie say, 'Don't bother us this morning, go clean something.'"

"I know this sounds like a broken record, but is this unusual?"

"Ya, ya, of course, that what I say to you. I mostly bring morning tea and a sweet treat at 9:00. On this day, early, they drink tea. Letty was upset. She cry, say, 'Oh dear, make much mess of everything, I not lock door.'"

"Okay, Letty was crying," Oliver was feverishly taking notes, "And she made a mess of things, didn't lock the door and what about Annie?"

"Miss Annie, 'That okay dear, it's not your fault. We be alright, no bad thing going to happen. Here now, drink tea, it will make you better.' I go to kitchen."

"This is interesting. It just might be the crack I've been looking for." *Listen to me. I'm getting as bad as the sisters, cracks and all.*

"Ya. Big crack!" Ulga smiled and nodded in agreement.

Oliver slid into the hot tub with a sigh of relief. *What a place, oh but to live the life of the well-off. Did she say twelve years? She should be able to speak better English by now.* He sat in the hot tub, looking through the glass wall. From where he was he could see the entire back half of the estate. The ground's keeper was trimming off the dead roses just outside. He could hear Mrs. Dustvaffor in the next room. "Oh Mrs. Dustvaffor, won't you keep me company for a few minutes?"

"Na. That plant bad for Ulga."

"What plant is that?" *Time to get out and go back to work. Where's my clothes? Oh, there they are over there.* Splashing water preceded him as he climbed out.

"You stand next to plant. I move, if I were you, she eat man."

"What? What are you talking about?"

The elderly man was rapping wildly on the glass from the

83

outside, hollering— "Get away from there! Get away from that there plant. It already ate the professor!"

"The plant ate O'Coins?" His eyes went wide in disbelief.

At this, Mrs. Dustvaffor disappeared. Oliver hurriedly dressed, as he pointed to the ground's keeper and—"I'm coming out. You stay put!" Leaving through the front, he hollered—"Mrs. Dustvaffor, where are you? Meet me outside. Now!" As he rounded the corner going toward the back of the house, Mrs. Dustvaffor and Harold Hoehandler were conversing in hushed tones but both were using a lot of frantic hand motions.

"We don't want any part of that room or that plant, Mr. Oliver."

"Calm down. Who did the plant eat?"

"Miss Annie and Miss Letty, they hushed it right up, but I know. I was here."

"Who got eaten?"

"Poor Professor Souser."

"You mean, he's missing too?"

"No, Charity and Annie pulled him free. Charity wanted to call a doctor, but Annie didn't want a doctor here, anyway Letty poured whiskey all over him and he revived straightway."

"When was this?"

"The day they christened the hot tub."

"No Sir, you're not going to get me in there. No way, No how," Harold stated empathetically, "no sir'ree," shaking his head as he walked away, gently pulling Ulga away from Oliver.

Oliver found the teacher at the college— "Are you Professor Souser?"

Looking over the rims of his glasses, he said, "Yes, I am, may I ask, to whom do I have the pleasure of speaking?"

"Sorry, I'm Detective Oliver S. Homes. I'm investigating the disappearance of Professor Penny O'Coins. I understand you're good friends."

"Aaaa, you might say that, conspirators in crime, at any rate."

"Crime, what do you mean by that?"

"Just an inside joke, we chase skirts together."

"So, we all skirt chase. What I'd like to know is, what were you doing at the Tower's Estate three days after graduation?"

"Three days after graduation," with a thoughtful frown, Professor Souser mulled this over in his mind, "That must have been the day I went looking for Penn."

"Tell me about it."

"I hadn't seen him in, yes, it was three days, wasn't it? And I thought maybe he and Letty . . ."

"He and Letty what?"

"Well, you know, he had been saying some pretty crazy things. He was sweet on Letty, maybe."

"Okay, so you went looking for your friend, so what happened up there. I've heard some things."

"So have I, but I really don't remember."

"Do you remember Jezebel?"

"So, there really is a . . . She really exists?"

"What are you trying to hide?"

"It's really embarrassing, do we have to discuss this?"

"Yeah, what if that plant ate O'Coins? They were real happy to hush it up for you, weren't they?"

"Naw, that's too weird, besides, Letty'd never keep that quiet. She has a thing for him, you know."

"I've heard that too. Okay, so tell me about your encounter with Jezebel."

"I had been drinking when I went out there, or I probably would never have gone, anyway, I must have gotten too close to that plant of Letty's. I'm told she tried to eat me."

"You don't remember?"

"I remember coming to on the floor with Charity and Annie going on like two chickens with their heads cut off—I was all wet and didn't have any feeling in my face. I remember Annie had her arm around me. She was upset."

"Okay, if you do think of anything, call me, or if you hear from him."

"Will do. I've half a notion he's off someplace camping or something, just getting school out of his system. We have to do that, you know. Actually though, he's supposed to show up for work. He has a summer job. You might want to check into that."

"Where?"

"The watch tower for fire watch."

"I will."

On his way back from the school, Oliver stopped off again at the Tower's Estate, just in time to see Annie and Letty pull into their drive.

"It's been a long time since I've seen a Studebaker, what a marvelous old car. You must be proud."

"Yes, she was the last thing Papa bought before he passed on. There certainly are a lot of memories tied up in her."

"Why Annie, you've never liked her color."

"And I suppose she has a name too?"

"Oliver, Meet Matilda. Perk up for Mr. Oliver, Matilda."

"Annie, I came with a purpose. I have to know about O'Coins. He was here the night after graduation. He was here, late, wasn't he?"

"We got home just about dark. He showed up shortly after that."

"Annie was awfully mad, she yelled at him! She ran him off."

"He was drunk! You bet I ran him off. I'm glad we've seen the last of him."

"Annie, don't you think he looks a little like Bartrum Sweetmiller?" Turning to Oliver, Letty continued, "Bartrum Sweetmiller used to be the gate keeper here. Papa let him go when we were teenagers. He's worked for the Bearzall Estate as the ground's keeper, ever since. Hummmm, I wonder if he still does. He might be dead, poor fella. He had a crack in his front tooth. Our gate is in such disrepair now that it's nearly nonexistent. This was a grand ole place once upon a time. I remember Bartrum as a young man. He had a crush on Annie. He was a bit older though. Then Annie went off to school. She was in England for two years. When she got back Bartrum wasn't with us anymore. I remember, he was always asking about her. He never married either."

This is getting me nowhere fast. "Letty, how well do you know Professor O'Coins?"

"We were going to buy a ranch."

"Do you think he would go off camping without telling anyone?"

"No, unless he was with her."

"Who?"

"The one on the broomstick, with the fly-away hair." Letty's eyes narrowed and with a determined set of jaw, she continued, "I'd like to put a crack in her broom! A permanent one! She'd never dance again."

"Who, Letty?"

"I wonder if Bartrum ever got his tooth fixed? He really wasn't all that bad looking, you know."

"Letty, who rides a broom?"

"Did I ever tell you about our flying carpet?"

CHAPTER 9

Harold Hoehandler and Ulga Dustoffer

A peek through a crumbling archway revealed a well manicured lawn, with small tufts of violets dotting the rich thick green. The fragrance of a thousand flowers mingling with the evergreens was evidence that spring flourished here. *Almost a fairy tale place,* thought the professor. *The two old ladies must have had quite a childhood here. I can almost see the wood nymphs and sprites and even a baby dragon or two, hiding beneath the giant weeping willows. Puck has visited and poured his love potion out on this secluded magical place.*

"Boo!"

"Oh Letty! I wasn't expecting to see you out here," said the startled Jonah Souser.

"It's beautiful, don't you think?"

"Yes."

"Would you like to walk with me?"

"Sure, I'd like that, besides, I'd like to talk to you. Perhaps you could tell me when you last saw Penn?"

"Oh, you mean Saturday night?"

"Yes, I think so."

"He came to see me and Annie ran him off."

"That's all?"

"No, actually he came back. See the trellis under my balcony?"

"Yes."

"Well, he climbed the trellis onto my balcony and spoke sweet words of love, 'Letty, Letty, wherefore art thou, my love?' I answered, 'I'm here, my beloved,' then something terrible happened."

Wide eyed, Souser asked, "What happened?"

"He fell . . . I keep telling everyone."

"Did you see him after that?"

"Yes, and he was all covered with dirt."

I smell a Letty story, "Has he called you since Saturday night?"

"You mean . . . on the phone?"

"That's generally the accepted way."

"No, he hasn't called me on the phone."

Musing to himself— "You don't suppose he really is dead?"

"Did you know," asked Letty, "That my Uncle Uly just disappeared in thin air? They never did find him. Most people think he fell into a hole and got buried while he was on a safari in South Africa."

"Thanks, really comforting. I think I'd better go now."

"Won't you stay? Annie'll be so sad that she missed you. I could fix some lemonade? Besides you haven't heard what really happened to Uncle Uly."

"Another time, Letty. Thanks." *No offense, but I've heard about your lemonade.*

Later that afternoon, Oliver rounded the corner and came to a stop in front of Tower's Estate. *What a grand old place. Imagine, the first time I saw this place, it really intimidated me. It could be a scene out of an old romance novel. Acres and acres of lawn, landscaped with trees from every continent and so many colorful flowers. I wonder who ever thought of all the different kinds of flowers planted here?* He spied Harold working in a flower bed about half-way to the house. *I think I'll just park here and walk up.*

"Hello! I've seen you here before, remember me?"

"Yes, you're the investigator that's been nosin around here. Find the bad guy yet?"

"Afraid not, Harold, you live on the grounds here, don't you?"

"Yes. I have the cabin out back. I've been working here for eight years now. The two fine elderly ladies hired me when nobody else would. They're real good to me."

"Do you take care of the plants inside too?"

"You mean the plants in the hot tub room? No, I told you before, I won't go near that room. They got a plant in there that eats professors. Like I told you before, one of the sisters' teacher friends almost got et by a plant in there. They feed it whole chickens sometimes, that's what I hear. Those are the only plants they have in the house. No! I don't go in that room."

"Have you ever seen Professor O'Coins here?"

"Several times here lately. I know he was here, one night last week. I saw his truck. Then he left about 3:00 in the morning, maybe a little after. I heard him get in his truck and slam the door. He had trouble starting it."

"Did you see him leave?"

"No, but I heard him."

"Do you know when he arrived?"

"No, but it was after dark, because I didn't get home until after dark. His truck wasn't here when I got home."

"Do you remember what Professor O'Coins' pickup looks like?"

"Sure do. That sweet little Jimmy. I'd give my eye teeth to get my hands on that. My cousin Wesley had one just like it. Same dirty green even. We took that rig into places a cat wouldn't go. James, my cousin called him. He made noises like a bull frog calling for his mate. Yes Siree . . . that was a four wheeler."

"Do you have any idea why he would be here that time of night?"

"Well, sometimes he comes to visit Miss Letty when Miss Annie is off to her night classes."

"At 3:00 in the morning?"

"That is odd, isn't it. Sometimes Miss Annie forgets the time when she's developing pictures with that other professor, but I've never known her to be past midnight, ever."

This is getting too weird. The whole pack of them are weird.

"Hello Letty. This is becoming a habit. A nice habit, though. May I come in?"

"Of course, Oliver. It's so nice to see you. Did you come to enjoy our hot tub, again?"

"Not this time. What a shame too, but I have business to take care of today. Is Miss Annie home?"

"She's writing letters, I think. Come on in, follow me." She led him through the house and out through the kitchen to the patio. Annie was sitting out on the patio engrossed in the business at hand. When she saw the two coming toward her, she laid her paperwork aside. "Oliver, what a pleasant surprise. Would you like something to drink?"

"Like a whiskey?" Letty was wearing a smug smile.

"No, no, please no. I have a waistline to watch," he said, patting his overabundance.

"Actually, I have something I want to discuss with you, Miss Annie. Last week, aaah, Saturday night, I believe, O'Coins' pickup was here until 3:00 in the morning. I need someone to shed some light on this. I'm trying to figure out why his pickup would be here on the night he disappeared."

"Saturday? Oh! That was the day Letty and I went on a picnic up on Tower Mountain. We got home after dark and soon after, Professor O'Coins showed up here, very drunk, demanding that we let him in the house. I told Letty not to let him in.

She hollered at him, 'Go away', she made me lock the door." Letty giggled and added, "He nearly fell down the steps, going down them backwards."

"Annie, were you home that night?"

"Of course, I was home."

"All night?"

"Of course, all night. Just exactly what is it that you want to know, Oliver?"

"Do you know why his pickup was here until 3:00 in the morning?"

"Perhaps he went for a walk around the lake to sober up, who knows! He was dead drunk."

"If he left after that, why was his pickup still here at 3:00 in the morning?"

"I don't know, maybe he walked home. He was terribly drunk. Maybe he came back later for the truck."

"Okay, well, I guess that's . . . no, it's not all, I want to take another look at that plant you have in there. What do you call that room?"

"Planet Venus. Isn't that quaint? Letty named it."

"Did she name that plant too?"

"As a matter of fact, she . . . Oliver, are you making fun at us?"

"Sort of, I suppose. A man eating plant named Jezebel. Forgive me, it is kind of way out! I don't think I know anyone else who names rooms and plants. Maybe I will stay, long enough to unwind in the hot tub."

Oliver was blowing at bubbles, absorbed in thought when Annie came in to join him. Right behind her, Letty asked, "May we join you or are you too busy in your mind?"

"Ah, come on in, the water's fine. Besides, I'm not thinking."

"Oh good, come on, Annie."

CHAPTER 10

Angela's Grandfather

"Well, I don't know where she is. I haven't seen her for a week!"

"Now, just a minute! Your only grandchild, she's been gone for a week and you're not worried?"

"Of course, I'm worried, now, get out of here and leave me alone!"

"Mr. Goldsworth, why haven't you called the police?"

"Get out!"

"No! I've got a missing professor and now a missing college student who just happens to be a dancer at the local night club where the professor spent a lot of time. It's time for some answers. What's going on? Do we have a people-eating monster on the loose?"

"I got this in the mail a couple of days ago," handing Oliver a piece of paper. It read—"Don't worry, Gramps, I'm alright. I'm outa here for a while. I'm going to hide away and study real hard. I have to get my grades up. I love you. I'll keep in touch."

"Where' the envelope?"

"It's here somewhere." Arthur Goldsworth sighed heavily as he shuffled papers. "Here it is," handing it to Oliver, then not turning loose— "Wait a minute! This isn't Angela's handwriting. I want to bring charges against O'Coins. That dirty so and so. I know he's kidnapped my granddaughter!"

"Now hold on Mr. Goldsworth. You don't know any such thing. Let go of this and I'll get it checked out. Then we can go from there." Oliver yanked the envelope out of his tightly gripping fingers. "Mr. Goldsworth, I am sorry your grand daughter is not here, but we don't know if she left on her own accord or if she had help." Oliver gently put a steadying hand on the older mans shoulder. "You take it easy. I'll let you know what I find out. In the mean time, is there someone I can call for you, do you need someone to talk to, a counselor?"

"I don't need anyone. Just find my granddaughter! You get out of here. Arthur Crabapple Goldsworth III doesn't need anyone!" he shouted as he pushed Oliver outside. Arthur Crabapple Goldsworth III slammed the door in Oliver's face.

"Mr. Goldsworth! Mr. Goldsworth! Do I have to kick your door down?" Oliver shouted.

The big oak door swung open, "We are finished, Sir!"

"No, Sir, we are not," Oliver shoved his foot in the door. "Calm down, Mr. Goldsworth, let's take you down to the station and discuss this with the mad, er . . . ah . . . I mean Madelynn Hatter."

"And who is this Madelynn Hatter?" Arthur Goldsworth sneered at Oliver.

"She's the Chief. If you want the police department to look for your granddaughter, you have to come down to the office and make out a report. I'll take you there, but you must calm down." He exhaled a long slow breath.

"I'll get my things."

"Mr. Goldsworth, do you have any proof your granddaughter was abducted? Do you have a recent picture of her?"

"I already told your detective everything. He has the fake letter, why aren't you out there looking for her? That dirty so and so took her and you are covering for him! I'll sue the whole lot of you! Find my granddaughter!" His voice went higher in pitch and his face turned an ugly red. "My driver is here. Find my granddaughter!" He jabbed a fat stubby finger into Oliver's chest and exited the police station, he turned and ranted "You better find that, that, O'Coins thing before I do!"

"That went well, don't you think?" Oliver sighed.

"Check out the handwriting of all her friends." Madelynn Hatter sputtered impatiently.

"I've already done that. No matches. We've hit a dead end on this."

"No, we haven't." She was still impatient. "Angela and O'Coins disappeared at the same time. This could be a simple case of a prolonged trip to Reno. Check O'Coins handwriting."

"You really don't think . . . ?"

"Yes, I do think, sometimes. Check it out!"

"Yes Sir!" Oliver made the necessary call to forensics. As he hung the phone up, he turned to Madelynnn, "This doesn't make sense. O'Coins was after Letty's money, why would he elope with Angela? I talked to Letty's lawyer. She was about to sign papers giving him power of Attorney over her half of the estate, so why would he marry someone else?"

"You mean Miss Letty thinks O'Coins is attracted to her?" Her face gave her astonishment away.

"Stranger things have happened. At any rate, he had her convinced that he cared for her or she wouldn't have been ready to sign on the dotted line."

The disappearance of Penny O'Coins was finally released to the media. Angela swallowed the last can of Pork N Beans in the supply cupboard slowly without chewing as the news came over the radio. Terrified and in desperate need of food and a change of clothing, she left the tower on foot.

She had gone for what seemed like miles and miles. Her feet were blistered and the left three inch heel had broken off. "He's gone, and left me here to rot! He's gone and got himself killed. I hate you! I hate you, Penny O'Coins!" In this hysterical condition, she walked down the gravel road for the better part of a day. Shortly before dusk, cold, tired, torn, and hungry, she sat on a dead log on the side of an endless road.

Oliver went back to the office to get his messages. Madelynn Hatter was waiting for him. "Where have you been?"

"I just came from the sisters."

"Plump, puckered, like a plum?"

"Oh, you've talked to them too!"

"Yes! I know all about the hot tub, the think tank, indeed! Have you even thought to try going to the tower? Have you been looking for Classie Acts, or are you spending all your time in that hot tub?"

"How do you know about Classie Acts?"

"I'm your boss. I know everything!"

"Good, maybe you can tell me where Classie Acts and the professor are!"

"I'd fire you if I could find a replacement. Even a half-wit would be an improvement. I want a written report on my desk by morning and you'd better have checked out the tower. Include those findings in your report."

"Yes Sir! Right on it, Sir!" *The mad hatter, at it again!*

Oliver started up the mountain road, but before he went far, he ran into a hysterical, disheveled young woman. He slid to an abrupt stop in the gravel.

"He left me up here, all alone . . . bears . . . and lions," she sobbed. "I'm going to kill him! If I ever find him, I'm going to kill him! The old ladies did something to him, he said so! They're after us. He said, 'Those two old ladies are going to kill us!'"

"Whoa! Calm down! Come on, everything's going to be okay. Here, have some water. Are you Angela?"

He sat, looking at a hot, overwrought, mosquito bitten, young woman who didn't at all remind him of a dancer. Her hair was mussed, her shorts and T-top were filthy and her face was made up with road dust and mascara smeared by tears. "Miss, are you Angela?"

"He went to see the old ladies," she said between sobs. "He said he'd be right back."

By this time Oliver was pretty sure he was talking to Angela. "Who? Who are you talking about?"

"I know they've done something to him." Babbling on, she seemed oblivious of being there with the detective. "Why did he leave me up here?"

She could have been talking to herself for hours, days even, she's out of it. He reached for his radio— "Bunnie, this is Oliver, come in, please."

"What's up Olie?"

"I've picked up an overwrought young woman on Tower Mountain Road. I believe her to be our missing Angela Goldsworth. Please get in touch with her grandfather, and have him meet us at the hospital. She looks as if she's suffering from exposure, perhaps dehydration and most assuredly hysteria. She keeps mumbling something like, 'The old ladies did it, the old ladies did it.' Get in touch with the Mad Hatter for me, will you? She can meet us at the hospital too."

It was getting dark now and Angela slumped beside him, curling herself into a fetal position all the way through town and the outlying suburbs to the hospital. She was still sobbing uncontrollably and shivering from freight. As they pulled in, her grandfather came to a screeching halt right next to them

Flinging the passenger's door on Oliver's car open, "Where in hades have you been? Do you have any idea what you've done to me? Talk to me, before I shake it out of you." He had her by the shoulders ready to carry out his threat.

Oliver intervened— "Mr. Goldsworth, please. She's not hearing you, please, let them take her inside. Sit with me while we wait to see what the doctor has to say."

Two orderlies came for her and took her inside. Mr. Goldsworth sat in silence, shaken and ashen white. From time to time, he would leave his chair and pace back and forth through the long hallway. The sterile smell only added to the unreal atmosphere; it was like stepping into another dimension where everything loses color and meaning.

The doctor approached Mr. Goldsworth, "You may go in and see her for a few minutes. I doubt that she'll know you. Given a little time, she'll be alright, but right now, she's really out of it. I've given her a sedative and we'll keep her here for a couple of days for observation."

In the wake of O'Coin's disappearance, the media devoured this story and the morning's headlines read, "Arthur Goldsworth III's granddaughter found alive. Her first words were, 'The old ladies did it.'"

"Newest information on the investigation into the disappearance of the professor Pen O'Coins links Angela Goldsworth to his sudden disappearance. Was she the last one to see him? Is he dead or alive?"

Professor Bearzall wandered down the corridor of the hospital wearing a thoughtful frown.

"Are you looking for someone, Sir?"

"Yes, I believe a Miss Goldsworth is here somewhere. Could you direct me in the right direction, perhaps? I'm her uncle."

"I believe she's down the next hall, three doors to the left. Room 312."

"Thank you so much," he said with a smile, turning to watch the way her white skirt swayed as she walked. Finding Classie was easy with the directions—"Hi, how are you doing sweetie?"

"Dr Bearzall, you've gotta get me out of here. Everyone thinks I'm crazy. The two old ladies killed him and they're going to kill me too."

"Whoa . . . slow down, who killed who?"

"They killed him. They caught us fixing my grade. You know, like we did?"

Professor Bearzall cleared his throat several times, loudly, and his red face shone brightly. "Shh," he said. "Do you want someone to hear?"

"I don't care who hears. I don't care if the whole world hears! I want out of here, now!"

"You stay put and be quiet and I'll see what I can do. okay?"

"Mr. Homes, this is Katherine Bearzall."

"Call me Oliver, Mrs. Bearzall. How can I help you?"

"Oliver, you said to call you if I should hear anything or remember anything. A week or so ago I saw Arthur

Goldsworth at the store."

"Does he usually do his own shopping?"

"I don't know. He was in the parking lot ranting at Penn. He was screaming, raving, like a lunatic, being real loud."

"What parking lot was this?"

"Why, Super Tower's Market, the only store in Tower Falls with a parking lot."

"Oh, oh yes. Did anyone else see him there? I mean, see him yelling at O'Coins?"

"Well, Classie was there and Penn. I think they were together, maybe, and let me see, oh yes, Father Paul and those two nuns who run the school. I never can remember their names, and Mrs. Dustvoffer, the sister's housekeeper, came out of the store before Father Paul got it broke up."

"What did Father Paul do to break it up?"

"He took Arthur Goldsworth by the arm. I think he said something to him, I'm not sure, I was just leaving. Classie got into the car with her grandfather and they left."

"You said Mr. Goldsworth was hollering at O'Coins. What did he say?"

"He wasn't just hollering at him, he was ranting 'I'm going to kill you! I'm going to kill you!' he was pretty mad."

"Mrs. Dustvaffor, do you remember a scene at the store between Arthur Goldsworth and Penny O'Coins?"

"Ya. Mr Goldworth was mad. Red face, he holler loud too!"

"Do you remember what he said?"

"Ya, 'I kill you,'" she said in her thick Scandinavian accent. "Ya, that is it, I kill you. You think he did?"

"I'm not supposed to think, Mrs. Dustvaffor. My boss doesn't like that. Tell me, when did this happen, do you remember?"

"A week after graduation, before the hot tub even. Ya, a week ago, Saturday, in the morning. Is the man O'Coins really gone?"

"I don't know, I hope not."

Dickie entered the Parish through the side door and hurriedly made his way to the front. He spied the priest with two alter boys going over their part in the morning service. Not waiting to see if they had finished, he intruded. "Father Paul, I need to speak with you."

"Of course. Do you have a confession?"

"I need to speak with you now."

Father Paul noticed his frown and the urgency in his voice.

"It's a matter of life and death," Dickie said.

"Go into my office, I'll be right there." He turned to the boys, "You two did a fine job today. I'll see you in the morning." The boys poked and scuffled with one another as they left. The priest scratched his close cropped hair looking after them before turning back to his study. As he entered the room, Dickie jumped to his feet holding out a newspaper clipping. "Here, I want you to see this."

Father Paul took the clipping and after a moment asked, "What does this murder have to do with you? You didn't do it, did you?"

"Of course not, you know me better than to ask that. But I know who did, that is, I took a picture of him. I'm in over my head this time, Randy. I need help."

"Don't ever call me by my given name. I'm Father Paul now."

Some time later, Dickie left the parish only to find Katherine waiting impatiently in the parking lot.

"Well, it's about time!"

"What are you doing here?"

"I should be asking you— "

"Scoot over!" Dickie climbed into the driver's seat. "Give me the keys. You didn't tell anyone where I went, did you?"

Katherine laughed out loud. "Of course— the man in the Hawaiian shirt," but she stopped laughing when Dickie turned white. "Hey! What's going on? First you sneak off without telling me where you're going and then you accuse me of telling what I obviously don't know."

He squealed out onto the street. "I told you and you didn't believe me the first time and you don't believe me now." They drove home in silence.

CHAPTER 11

Bearzall Falls In

"Father Paul, I'm Detective Oliver S. Homes. I'm investigating the disappearance of Penney O'Coins."

"Oh yes, the professor. I saw the man in the parking lot at the store some time ago, a week ago maybe. Yes, the older gentleman was furious. He should have his blood pressure checked, poor man."

"Was he hollering at the professor?"

"Yes, something like, 'I'm going to kill you!' Before the others saw what was going on, he was waving a handgun around, I got it away from him. I gave it back after he calmed down. I hope he didn't carry through with his threat. I would never forgive myself. Sister Mary Ruth and Sister Mary Sarah were with me. I can call them in if you would like to speak with them."

"I think I have what I need for now. Perhaps later I will need to speak with them. Thank you for your time."

"Here, I'll show you out. Do you go to church, Oliver?"

"No, Father, I don't."

"I didn't think I'd seen you here. We'd love to see you for services. Please consider this a personal invitation."

"Thank you, Father."

"Bunnie, put your ears on . . . come in, come in?"

"Oliver, I have been trying to reach you. The Mad Hatter left for the day. Your time is your own now. Meet me out at the Buzzard's Branch."

"Sorry Bunnie, I wish I could. I have to talk to the Tower girls again this afternoon. Maybe if I can get away early enough, I'll wander out that way. Anyway, tell Barbie 'Hi' for me, okay?"

"Sure thing, over and out."

Oliver wandered around for a while trying to fit the pieces together. He found himself up on the look-out road again. He kept thinking maybe if he retraced his footsteps he could see things more clearly, but it didn't help. He finally pulled up in front of the old manor and greeted the lion head with a salute— "I'll bet you could tell me a story or two, old friend. Who did it, anyway? What happened to the professor? Still not talk'n, huh?"

"Is that you, Oliver? Did I hear you talking to yourself?"

"You sure did, Ma'am, maybe Mr. Lion Heart will whisper in my ear and tell me the secret of this little who-done-it-tale." Oliver was trying to draw Letty into one of her stories. He needed something to ease the tension. There was this terrible pain starting in the back of his neck and circling all the way around his head. It felt like an iron band tightening its grip on him.

"You need to get away for a few days, Oliver. Did I ever tell you about our trip to Niagra Falls? Here, get comfy and I'll tell you all about it."

"I'm all ears, Letty."

"Papa had hired another nanny . . . and then he decided Annie and I needed to see America's greatest natural waterfall firsthand. I think that was because we were always playing up at Tower Falls on Sparrow Mountain and Annie told him it was so beautiful. She said it was her favorite spot in all the world. He didn't know about the cave behind the falls, anyway, I'm getting off track. Where was I? Oh yes, Niagra Falls. Our new nanny bought a wooden barrel and was trying to take us over the falls but Papa caught hold of Annie and I by our arms and yanked us out of the barrel. He

104

was unable to get hold of our nanny and she went sailing over the falls and was buried alive under all that water . . . Alive!"

"She went over the falls? Did the authorities find her?" Oliver was obviously caught up in Letty's tale.

"No, just like Wee Willy, buried alive, and the authorities haven't found him either, isn't that ironic?"

"Letty, are you telling stories again?" Neither Letty nor Oliver had heard Annie enter the room and were startled by her voice. "Here you two, I've fixed us grinders for lunch. Eat hearty, Oliver. Would you like some tea with your lunch?"

"What's a grinder?" asked Oliver.

"The same thing as a hero sandwich, or . . . sub, I think they're called?"

"After lunch," Letty added, "We can hold a meeting of our new Think Tank Club, okay?"

I wonder when people started being buried alive in Letty's stories? Oh! Oh no! Was Penny O'Coins still alive when we buried him? Her face went pale at this thought.

"Are you alright, Miss Annie?"

"Yes, yes, I'm fine. I was just faint for a bit. I'm starved, that must be it."

Professor Bearzall saw the two old ladies down at the lake and his imagination slipped into overdrive. He couldn't get Angela's words out of his mind. Later at the party thrown in honor of Jonah's national recognition for his photography accomplishments, there was talk of his friend Penny O'Coins and his disappearance and numerous conclusions as to what might have happened to him. He convinced Jonah Souser to go to the lake with him and the two of them left, looking for their friend. At the lake's edge, there was an exchange of words and Jonah Souser could be seen walking up Rainbow Drive toward his house.

The inebriated Professor Bearzall stood on the peer alone. Equipped with a six pack of beer and a sweater, he climbed into the small row boat and maneuvered it out into the lake. Rowing aimlessly on this clear night, he didn't even notice the half moon which lit the lake just enough to cast an eery shadow. "Where are you, you SOB, I know they bumped you off. Annie found out about your little scheme which I might add, my friend, was working extremely well. Letty was to meet with Lyer to sign the final papers, tomorrow." Pausing long enough to catch his breath, he was sure he saw bubbles escaping from the darkened depths. In his drunken stupor he assimilated an Elizabethan tongue—"Doth thee speak to me from thy watery grave, oh foul knight? Thy fair maiden's keeper hath guessed your guise." Standing up suddenly, he thrust one hand to his heart and the other, wildly in the air, proclaiming— "I shall avenge your sad and brutal demise." The boat began to rock and in his drunken condition he went headlong into the water. The six-pack of beer teetered precariously and then beer and boat both overturned. His sweater floated for a moment— a solute to the personage of Professor Richard Bearzall, and then, slowly sank.

From the Tower's balcony, Letty watched through a hazy mist as bubbles, lots of bubbles, came up from the deep blackness. They surrounded the little row boat Professor Bearzall was standing in. Mystified and entranced by the scene she was witnessing, she stood, wide-eyed, staring at the lake. She watched in horror as a giant frog came out of the water and grabbed the professor by the leg and pulled him under. The boat rocked, violently and then overturned, six-pack and all. She watched until the bubbles slowly crossed the lake and disappeared into the shadows. Letty rubbed her eyes and looked over toward the lights across the lake again, "This little froggie . . . he went a courtin . . . ah ha, ah ha, this little froggie . . . he went a courtin. This little froggie isn't a courtin, oh my goodness—Jonah, go back and help! No, no, little sister, you never get anything right. I can't tell anyone about this—It didn't happen. Annie! Annie! Come here!"

Annie came running and was out of breath when she reached the balcony. "Letty, what is it?"

"Oh, what a dream! I just had the strangest dream."

"You're white as a sheet!"

"Don't go, Annie. Can we have that slumber party now? Please stay with me."

Annie crawled under the covers as Letty, paled and

shaking, asked, "Do you want to hear my dream?"

"I don't remember when I dreamed last, tell me."

"It was really foggy like, but it was on the lake. There was a row boat. One guy refused to get in and the other man was throwing his arms around and hollering—"

"What was he hollering?"

"I don't know. I couldn't hear— the fog was too thick, like in a horror story. It was so scary—"

"What happened then?"

"It cleared a bit around the boat. There were bubbles everywhere— the music said something terrible was happening. Then a giant frog came out of the water and grabbed the man in the boat, and then he was gone, and that was the end of my dream."

Annie was unable to go to sleep so she slipped quietly out of Letty's bed and went for a walk by herself. She walked down by the lake and found her favorite bench. She sat there for quite a while trying to piece some things together. *What is going on?* She pondered. *Letty hasn't been herself for a while. Something's going on that she's not telling me about.* "Hello Jonah, you startled me."

"I didn't mean to. I was just walking, actually, I came back to check on Dickie. He probably thinks I'm mad at him."

"What happened?"

"He wanted me to get in the row boat with him."

"In his condition?"

"Exactly. Anyway, I went home, but I couldn't sleep. Want to walk around the lake with me? I don't see him anywhere. He must have gone home."

"Why not, I can't sleep either."

"Good morning, big sister. Did you sleep well?"

"Like a baby."

"You don't get off this easy— you have to tell me what happened. Did anything happen? You know! Did it?"

"What are you talking about?"

"I saw you two, last night— don't try to tell me that wasn't you and Jonah. I know it was."

"Then you know what happened."

107

"I went to bed. I didn't snoop."

"We walked around the lake— I just supposed you were watching. You were, weren't you?"

"No, after I saw who it was, I went to bed."

"We walked— and held hands."

"Nothing more? Is that all?"

"He said he felt like we were souls mates."

"That's heavy!"

"I think we connected."

"This is so exciting! Did he do anything?"

"What do you mean?"

"You know what I mean! Did he kiss you? Did he ask to see you again? Come on, big sister, fess up!"

"There isn't anything to confess. He has the nicest smile."

"What were you doing down at the lake last night, Annie?" Oliver sat down between the two ladies.

"We were looking for the missing professor, of course."

"We?"

"She and Jonah, who else?" Letty added.

Oliver decided to pass on that remark and turned back to Annie." What makes you think he's in the lake?"

"Actually, I was watching the bats. I do that quite often this time of the year." Annie had a far off look on her face. "I miss those days— it's been too long."

"You do what?"

"Watch the bats eat at dusk," added Letty, "We used to do that with Papa. Those were happy carefree days, when we were children. They whiz and whirr, and they dip and dive. They're after the bugs on the water's surface. This year is a good year. The bats are plentiful and very fat." She looked at Oliver with a sparkle in her eye.

Laughing eyes. She must have been beautiful when she was younger. What a beautiful shade of green. I've never seen eyes so green, wait a minute! Letty doesn't have green eyes! oO, okay, they change color when she's story-telling.

"Did you want to hear about Penn?"

"Well, yes, Letty, tell me about Penn."

"He grabbed me, you know, passionately. He was kissing me, and Annie was jealous."

"Letty, you know that's not true." Annie was exasperated.

108

"It could have been, if you'd have left us alone."

"I'm certainly not jealous!"

"Are too!"

"Am not!"

"Ladies, please!" *Oh no! Not this again!*

"That's what caused the crack that goes from east to west."

"North to South!"

"Ladies, please! Just sit down and be quiet!" Oliver raised his voice in desperation and the color in his face rose as well.

"Oh dear, Annie, I think he means it. Would you like a story to calm you down? You know, Oliver, our Papa wasn't the only one who traveled a lot. Great Grandpapa came West and made his fortune during the gold rush. He was captured by the Indians and the chief's beautiful daughter helped him escape. The mighty warriors chased them the length of the plains and then were trampled by the white buffalo. Great Grandpapa and his Indian princess escaped to the Rockies. That's how he came to discover our little valley here. He built this house for his Indian Princess and when she was homesick for her wild home, he took her to see the falls because she loved them so much."

"That's a beautiful story, Letty. Annie, I need to talk to Letty, but I am so hungry. Do you think you could whip up a sandwich while we talk?"

"What a grand idea," said Letty. "We can have lemonade with our sandwiches, come on, let's fix lunch together."

"Perhaps just tea!" *Please, no lemonade! I wonder what she can do to tea?*

"Letty, let's let Annie fix everything this time, okay?"

As Annie left the room, Oliver turned to Letty who had already opened her mouth to tell another tale, "The crack that goes North and South has a reason too, Oliver. Do you know why?"

"No, Letty, why?"

"Well, that's because of the war between the North and the South. There was a young soldier from the North who was wounded in battle. They thought he was dead and buried him. Well, he wasn't dead and during the night, he dug his way out of the shallow grave and a beautiful southern bell

109

found him and hid him in a secret room behind her closet until the danger had passed."

With a sigh, Oliver decided to try a different approach.

"You and me are pretty good friends by now, aren't we?"

"I just feel like I've known you all my life . . ." laughing out loud she added, "Well, half my life, anyway, you're not that old."

"Letty, we need to talk, I've heard you mention the name Wee Willy. Who is Wee Willy?"

"Why, my lover, of course."

"Are you trying to tell me that Penny O'Coins is Wee Willy?"

"Yes, I named him Wee Willy after, you know?"

"I'm going to stay away from that one! Letty, I'm going to ask you something really, really important. This could mean we could crack the case right now."

"The crack in the hot tub?"

"No, Letty, we're looking for Wee Willy."

"And I keep telling you, he caused the crack."

Oliver sat back in his chair in resignation— *where do I go from here?*

"Here we go! Turkey and cheese. I even have tomatoes and onions. And olives, Oliver, do you like olives? I have peperoncnes too, do you like hot peppers? I'll get some."

"This is perfect, nothing more please."

"After we eat, we can retire to the hot tub."

"Yes, and we could discuss Wee Willy and the crack."

"It's already late, ladies, and I have to report back to the office. Besides, my boss doesn't like your hot tub. I think she has something against cracks." All three laughed knowing the joke belonged to them.

"This reminds me of the time Papa called us from Arabia. Annie and I were teenagers by then. We were eating turkey and cheese sandwiches when the phone rang. It was Papa. He called to ask us what we wanted him to bring back from Arabia for us. Annie wanted a flying carpet and I wanted a magic lamp. When Papa came home, sure enough, he had a flying carpet, even with instructions on how to fly it. I still have the lamp he brought home for me. It's a beautiful lamp, but I never got my genie and Annie's carpet flew away and

110

was never seen again."

"I've always been interested in magic lamps and flying carpets," Oliver mused. "This is a delicious lunch, Annie, you have a magic touch when it comes to turkey and cheese. I hate to eat and run, but duty calls."

"I don't hear anything," said Letty, wide-eyed.

By this time, Oliver knew his way out and could hear the two ladies, still laughing as he left through the front door. He didn't notice the beauty or the sweet smell of Spring as he hurried to his car. Once there, he immediately rang for the office. Madelynn had been out earlier. This time, he reached her. "Madelynn, I spoke with Father Paul this morning. He and Mrs. Dustvaffor confirm Mrs. Bearzall's story. It's safe to say Arthur Goldsworth did threaten O'Coins in the parking lot."

"Have you talked to Goldsworth yet?"

"No, he's out of town until tomorrow, some sort of convention. He took his granddaughter with him."

"This whole investigation is going in the wrong direction, Oliver. It's uncovering more questions than answers. Something better break real soon! You have your assignment. Check back with me in the morning if nothing else breaks."

"Who do I talk to about my granddaughter's grades! If I'm going to be paying for her school, her grades better be good."

"Mr. Goldsworth, how was your trip? I'll get someone here right away for you to talk to," came the reply from the receptionist.

"And I intend to see to it that she gets the best instruction this college has to offer."

"Yes Mr. Goldsworth. All our instructors are hand picked for their positions. We have some of the best minds available here at Tower Falls College. Mr. Goldsworth, this is Ima Guide, Head of Counseling. Mrs. Guide will talk to you."

"Yes, well, I just want to make sure my granddaughter, Angela Goldsworth, is getting my money's worth."

"Hello, Mr. Goldsworth, I'm glad to meet you. Let's go into my office and pull her grades up on screen. Do you have her permission to see her grades?"

"I'm her legal guardian until she's twenty one and it's my money paying the bill here, I don't need her permission."

The receptionist was busy getting the main office while Mrs. Guide made small talk with the distraught man. "It is our policy to keep our bigger contributors happy," she was told. "Be nice to him and give him anything he wants, within reason. After that point, I don't know what to tell you, and, you didn't hear this from me."

"Mrs. Guide, I'm sorry to interrupt. Mr. Goldsworth can have the information he's looking for, I got special clearance from the office."

"Thank you, Daphne. That'll be all. Mr. Goldsworth, my screen shows your granddaughter on the honorable mention list."

"That's more like it. Thank you, Mrs Guide. I like people who are expedient. It's nice to know that the people here know what they're doing."

"Have a good day, Sir," she said as she walked to the main entrance with him. As she returned, Daphne stopped her.

"Can you believe that man?"

"Really overbearing, isn't he?"

"If the things I've heard about Angela are true, I can hardly blame her."

"There true."

"You mean, she really is a strip tease dancer?"

"She really is."

"It came out in the paper that she was in the hospital. Was it serious?"

"I don't know. She was in the hospital and Professor O'Coins is still missing, last I heard. Maybe she's in over her head, this time."

"What do you mean?"

"Professor O'Coins isn't the only teacher she's messed around with, how do you think she has the grades she does?"

"Are you serious?"

CHAPTER 12

Souser Falls In

Annie came out of the pantry at a dead run, through the dining area into the living room. *I must get a second phone . . . I'm not as young as I used to be.* "Hello?"

"Miss Annie, the is Iona Book, from the library. I have an over-due notice here on a book Letty checked out. Is she around?"

"No dear, she's feeding her pets right now. May I take a message?"

"Okay. Tell her, her book is over-due. She either needs to bring it in or come in and renew it."

"Okay, I'll tell her. By the way, what is the name of the book?"

"Ten Easy Steps to Home Taxidermy."

Annie nearly lost her wind— "Oh, okay." As she hung up, Annie turned to see if Letty had come in yet— "Letty! Come here!"

"Just a minute, Annie, Jezebel isn't finished yet . . . I'll be right in." As Letty came in, she was talking to herself. "Jezebel is getting so picky, ever since Professor Souser, she acts so stand-offish, she won't even eat. Do you know, I think she's got Annie-itis, maybe she's stuck on him too."

"I want to see the book you checked out."

"Oh, but I'm not through with it yet. Do you know, Jezebel won't eat heart or liver, or kidney. Organ meat is very good for her and no one else in the house will eat it either."

"Letty, the book!"

"Just a minute, shall we have a rump roast tonight? Mrs. Dustvaffor wants to know so she can put it on before she leaves."

"Who bought organ meat?"

"I did. It's good for us, besides, it was on sale."

"That was Iona Book. She wants to know if you are going to renew your book, it's over due."

"Yes, I'll renew it, I'm not through with it yet." Talking to herself again, "He didn't like organ meat either, he didn't want his."

What in the world is she up to? You don't suppose she's stuffed O'Coins? Maybe that is why the crack's there.

"Annie, maybe you should go lay down. You look awfully peeked. You go lay down and I'll bring your supper up."

"No supper, dear, just bring me some Alky-Seltzer."

Early Saturday morning, Letty was back in Annie's room to check on her sister, who, after a good night's sleep looked quite well. "I want to go rafting!"

"Rafting, Letty, we're supposed to be at the square today for the rally, remember?"

"I haven't forgotten. I told Father Paul we'd be there this afternoon. That leaves us all morning to go rafting, besides, you never know what you'll catch out on the river."

"I don't know, it might be a bit much."

"Hemingway went rafting, Annie, if you want to be a writer, you have to go rafting."

"I only write poetry."

"Oh, Annie, please! We can be Queens floating down the Nile, just like, out of Agatha Christie's 'Death on the Nile.' We can pretend that we saw a murder and the murderer knows we saw and we're running away. Won't that be fun? Better than sitting in the hot tub with a crack, going nowhere."

"Okay Letty, I guess we haven't had enough murder in our lives lately, but, wait, we don't know how to operate a raft, have you thought of that?"

"Oh yes, we'll use our imagination. Oh I can hardly wait.

We have to get ready. I'm going to wear my pearl Tierra, my three strand pearl necklace and earrings, my burgundy gown, the pink feathered boa and my pink shoes." She paused for a breath before continuing, "We can even wear make-up. I'm so excited!"

"Queens for a day, huh? Letty, where are we going to get a raft and the equipment we need?"

"It's all ready to go. It's all set up, even a book of instructions, and I packed a lunch. Aren't you proud of me?"

"Yes little sister, you've thought of everything."

Once on the river, the two ladies sat proudly in their rubber raft, floating down the "River Nile," like two proper ladies on a Sunday afternoon outing. They were decked in gown and full plumage. Letty, in her burgundy tiered Queen Ann's lace attire and Annie in mint silk and Georgette with a tiara, choker and earrings of smoky emeralds.

As they were floating the tranquil Nile, a scene was developing just around the bend in the rapids. Jonah Souser, an avid fisherman, dressed in full gear, straight from "Fish RUs," hooked the biggest fish of his fishing career. As he played his prize, he slipped and landed prone in the water. His hip boots quickly filled with water. He struggled with the boot's suspenders, holding the waist high boots in place with one hand while desperately clinging to the fishing rod with the other. The force of white water strength caught him, pulling him, thumping and bumping, down the rapids. Choking, gasping, spitting water, and trying to stay afloat nearly became a losing battle.

"Look Letty, what is that up ahead?"

"It looks like a head."

"Smarty!"

"I would even suppose it's attached. Oh my goodness, it's the professor."

"Hurry Letty, we've got to catch him. We've got to pull him out!"

As they caught up with the drowning fisherman, Letty yelled excitedly— "Grab him by the heels, Annie. That way we can dump the water and get him in the raft easier."

"No Letty!" Gasping for breath, the professor clung to the raft. "Help me with the suspenders."

"But then you'll lose them."

"I don't care!"

"I have a knife, I can cut them?"

"No!"

Both ladies, wet to the skin now—pulled and tugged on the professor as he was being battered by the passing rocks. All of a sudden the suspenders gave way, snapped with a vengeance and caught him in the face. He lost his hold on the raft and began to float down the rapids. The ladies managed to catch him again and this time, were able to pull him into the raft. With the boots gone and the hazardous rescue completed, he laid face down in the raft for a few minutes until he was able to get a second wind. Then he pulled himself to a sitting position— "Damn! I've lost everything!"

"You're alive and you weren't buried alive, either."

"My fish! My pole! My creole! My boots! All my tackle!"

"What were you trying to tackle?"

"Just the biggest fish I've ever had on a line."

"That's the biggest line I ever heard!"

"Letty behave! The man almost drowned."

"Might I interject here ladies. I think I'm going to be depressed for a few days."

Oliver was busy cleaning papers on his desk when the phone rang. "Hello?"

"Mr. Homes, this is Katherine Bearzall. We spoke yesterday, I'm really worried, my husband left here last night and hasn't returned."

"Does he do this often?"

"He's never stayed away over night before."

"Mrs. Bearzall, your husband drinks heavily, doesn't he?"

"Yes, but he always comes home."

"Was he drinking last night?"

"Yes, we were celebrating Jonah Souser's National Recognition Award."

"Do you know where your husband went?"

"No, I didn't know he was gone until this morning. I went to bed. I had a terrible headache."

"Who else was at the party last night?"

"Just about everyone. A National Recognition Award is a big deal in photography circles, a cause for celebration in any circle. With my head pounding the way it was, I really didn't pay much attention. When Dickie and Jonah left, I went to bed. I guess everyone was still here for awhile."

"Give me some names."

"Well, Charity and her husband and the Prints."

"How about Souser?"

"Yes, he was still here. I just said they left together. He and Dickie were having a contest earlier, to see who could down the most."

"Mrs. Bearzall, I've heard rumors about your husband, perhaps the pool finale isn't the only caper accredited to his accomplishments."

"If you're referring to the coeds, I know all about that. There wasn't an eighteen year old present last night, I made sure of that. There was no finale last night either "

"Are you sure no one showed up after you went to bed?"

"I'm positive, Dickie knows better than to bring any of his conquests home with him and besides, the only one involved with him at the moment disappeared with Penn and isn't she still in the hospital?"

"No, I believe she's home now, anyway, this gives me something to work with, if you think of something else, give me a ring. And Mrs. Bearzall, don't worry. He's probably just coming to someplace and trying to decide how to make it home without being caught. Okay? Be sure and give me a call when he shows up."

Oliver pulled up in front of the Buzzard's Branch, just as Joe was unlocking the front door.

"Hey detective, found your missing professor yet?"

"No Joe, I haven't. It seems we may have two professors missing now."

"You don't say. Now who's disappeared?"

"Bearzall, have you seen him?"

117

"Not since yesterday afternoon. He said he was throwing a party. It sounded like a real 'all-out' affair. Hey, I hear he strips and jumps in that fancy pool naked, has anyone said anything about that?"

"Yeah, the pool finale."

"Must be quite a sight, seeing a distinguished college president naked. How elite do you have to be to get in on one of these bashes?"

"I think I'm supposed to ask the questions."

"Fire away!"

"Have there been any whispers among the employees here. Is anyone speculating about Classie and O'Coins?"

"Well, you know. I think the general consensus is that the old man probably scared him clear outa town. Maybe he took Classie with him."

"Wait a minute, Joe, haven't you heard? Classie was in the hospital. She spent the week hiding out on Tower Mountain in the look out. She said O'Coins took her there to hide her and left her there. He never went back for her."

"Do you suppose that old man really did kill him like he said he was going to do?"

"What?"

"Why, in here, graduation night, the old man, you know, Classie's grandfather came storming in, pulled Classie off O'Coins lap and threatened to kill him if he ever saw him again. The whole place heard him and it was jam packed in here that night. Classie had just finished her famous number."

"What's that, her famous number, anything like Bearzall's?"

"Naw, she leaves this cute little string bikini on, but she might as well be naked, couldn't show any more. The crowd loves it. We have a full house every time she dances and you can bet, O'Coins is always here, front row center, but you know she's just a toy for him. He's really after the old woman's money. He'd even marry the old broad for her money."

"How do you know this?"

"You give that man enough to drink, he spills everything, that's what conceit does to a man, besides, I'm the

118

bartender, I hear everything. Don't you ever watch TV?"

Oliver laid a twenty on the bar, "Yeah, my boss says I watch too much TV and spend too much time in hot tubs."

"What's that for?"

"Drinks!"

"You didn't drink anything."

"Better give me a soda, have any root beer? Make it to go. I'll keep in touch," then left with his root beer. "Bunnie, this is Oliver, put your ears on, do you copy?"

"You're coming in loud and clear, Olie, what do you need?"

"Plug me through to the Mad Hatter."

Bunnie snickered before answering, "Olie, my friend, you're going to get yourself in trouble again, hatters wear ears too."

"Just do it! It's going to be a long day."

"Oliver, where have you been all morning? You forgot to check in. I've been looking for you. There's an overturned row boat in the South end of Duck Lake. Some kids were playing down there. One of the mothers called the police this morning to report it. I've been watching the scanner all morning to catch what's happening, check into it, now!"

"Don't you want to hear what I've got?"

"Make it quick!"

"Richard Bearzall's missing, or at least, he didn't come home all night."

"Oh fine, another missing professor, do you think?"

"Maybe, or maybe he tied one on. According to the bartender at the Buzzard's Branch, the three professors do that every once in a while."

"But this makes two professors now. I'm beginning to smell something fishy, I wonder."

"Ducky would be more like it, the lake's full of them! Anyway, I'm going to talk to Charity Townsend. Both she and her husband were at Bearzall's party last night. Perhaps they can shed some light on what's happening around here."

"Don't bet on it! I still smell a fish!"

Charity was out in her yard pulling weeds in a flower bed as Oliver pulled into her driveway. She waved, smiling,

"Come on in. I'll wash my hands and put the tea pot on. Any news to relate yet, Mr Homes?"

"Call me Oliver. Everyone does."

"Okay, Oliver. I'd like to talk to you. Letty said the strangest thing to me."

"What was that?"

"She was telling me that no one likes organ meat, not Annie, not Jezebel, not Mr. Hoehandler, not even Penn."

"Okay, Charity. I don't understand. What is this supposed to mean?"

"Well, she's referring to Penn in present tense."

"Okay, she's out of it, what else is new? Tell me something I don't already know."

"Okay, how's this? She showed me her book on taxidermy." She watched as Oliver turned pale.

Then he spoke, "They take major organs out when they stuff, don't they?" He was staring absentmindedly at the singing tea pot. Somehow, it seemed to melt the current train of thought and set another in gear. "I understand you and your husband were at the Bearzall's party last night?"

"Yes," she answered with a frown. She was trying to keep up with his mental hop-scotch. "We normally don't go, but this one was a little different. Professor Souser is really good to me. He's a special man and we wanted to help him celebrate."

"So, normally you don't drink?"

"We didn't drink last night, either."

"Were you still there when Bearzall and Souser left?"

"Oh yes, quite a surprising turn of events. We left right after that."

"Did Professor Bearzall leave after the pool finale?"

"He and Souser left together. There was no finale."

"So, you saw them leaving. Were they on foot?"

"Yes. They were walking down toward the lake. There was a beautiful moon, but I doubt either of them were in any condition to notice."

"Were they arguing?"

"Why no, I believe they were singing."

"Okay, Charity, if you think of anything that might help me to locate either O'Coins or Bearzall, would you give me a

120

ring?"

"Dr. Bearzall's missing too?"

"Maybe. At this point, we're not sure. He didn't come home last night. Holy mackerel! I forgot. I have to go. I'm supposed to check out an overturned row boat."

"Oh my gosh! I'm the one who reported the row boat. Was Professor Bearzall in that boat? What is going on?"

After Oliver left, Charity pondered over the recent happenings. She was remembering Penn's words from the previous week. He made a point of telling her, "*You do know I have special feelings for Miss Letty, don't you?*" *Was he trying to tell me something? Was this part of what's going on now? What am I supposed to do now? Maybe I could talk to Miss Letty? Maybe I should talk to her, after all, we're good friends.*

Charity drove up the long driveway to the Towers Estate. Sitting there, she wondered how she would approach Letty. After a few minutes, she went to the door and pulled the chain on the lion head. No answer. Again, she rang, but still no answer. *I wish I had the nerve to go in. What would I look for? No, this is crazy! Annie and Letty wouldn't harm a flea. Why can't I just let it go? I wouldn't want to find anything.* She got back into her car and drove down to the lake. For a while, she sat there drinking in the peacefulness and watching the water lap at the edge near the opposite bank. Then, too soon, she remembered the festivities in town.

The town square was cobblestone framed with small shops among the trees. An expanse of lawn surrounded the square and disappeared between the shops. The falls stood in magnificent splendor at the far end of the square. Man-made with cobblestones and cement, it was a replica of the original on Sparrow Mountain. It stood thirty feet high with ferns and moss growing as if it had always been that way. The water cascaded thirty feet to the bottom creating a pool which was enclosed with a cobblestone wall fifteen inches high and twelve inches through.

Letty danced the parameter of the pool on the cobblestone wall. Children delighted her and it wasn't long before she had an audience standing wide-eyed, listening to another story as she spun out her yarn. "I saw Fred Astaire dancing in the rain with Gene Kelly. They were dancing for Grace Kelly, the most beautiful woman ever, next to Marilyn, that is. Her beauty entranced Fred Astaire as he danced up to her like this," She pirouetted and bowed and held out her hand to a young girl standing near her. "And he took her hand and they danced away into the sunset."

Charity had been watching from a distance. As Letty reached a break in her story telling, Charity approached her — "Letty, you do that so beautifully, you must practice a lot. Do you practice on your balcony?"

"Why yes, every night. My favorite's Rachmananov, but I like to dance to all of the 19th Century classics and even, perhaps early 20th Century, like Arthur Fiedler and the Boston Pops, at least some of his earlier stuff. Are you interested in the dance?"

"Well, actually I'm interested in music, but this is a little before my time, besides what I would really like to know . . . were you dancing the night Professor Bearzall disappeared?"

"Have they found him yet?"

"No, I don't think so."

"When they do find him, they'll find his beer too. It should be nice and cold now. I have to go. My pets are hungry. They don't like organ meat. Oh, but I told you that already."

"But Letty!"

"Bye dear."

Annie sat at a table in front of the café drinking iced tea and enjoying the scene in front of her. "Charity, won't you join me?"

"Only for a moment, I want to go over and toss coins into the fountain. It will seem different with Father Paul gone won't it?"

"Gone? He's disappeared too?" Annie turned white. "What's going on?"

"Oh, no, Annie! Father Paul is going on a sabbatical. He will be announcing it soon."

"Whew! You really scared me. How long is he going to be gone, do you know?"

"Maybe six months, maybe a year, he needs the rest."

"What'll happen to the church with Father Paul gone?"

"We will have an interim priest. Father Paul assures me he will be here soon. I'll see you later, Annie. Have fun."

The falls formed a natural boundary between the square and the student recreation area, and was a favorite spot for many of the students. Even during the summer, the center was bustling with activity.

Jonah Souser happened by carrying a manila envelope. "Hello Annie, We meet again, huh?"

"Jonah, my, you do look the worst for wear. That's quite a shiner. Poor dear, you look terrible."

"Gee, thanks! I guess maybe I do owe you a 'thank you' you saved my life, you and Letty. I am grateful."

"I am too. With Professor O'Coins missing, we need you desperately, don't we? The college, I mean."

"You haven't heard about Professor Bearzall yet, have you?"

"Why no. What about him?"

"He's disappeared, too!"

"Are you serious?"

"Yes, Katherine called me just before I came in here, just a little while ago. Dickie apparently didn't go home last night after I left him at the lake."

"Oh my gosh! I hope he's alright."

"Me too! I have a really weird feeling about all of this. Something's just not right. Last night when we were walking, I felt like we weren't alone."

"I know, we both kept looking back, expecting to see someone else there. And you said you came back to check on him."

"Yes, when he wasn't there, I supposed he'd gone home. I hope he crawled off somewhere to sleep it off, but you'd think he'd have gone home by now."

"How many people are we going to lose before this stops?"

"What do you mean?"

"I heard Father Paul's leaving."

"I'm sorry to hear that. By the way, I've just come from photography. I picked up my pictures, would you like to see?"

"Yes." Annie drew her breath in as she took the pictures from his hand. "Oh, this is beautiful. Why this is our own falls, from across on the other mountain. You took this from a spot just below the look-out tower, didn't you?"

"Yes, are you familiar with that area?"

"Why yes, Letty and I were picnicking there recently. As a matter of fact, the day after graduation. It seems we may have been very near the tower the day Professor O'Coins took Angela up there."

"I still can't get over that. It seems so unreal. I can't believe that he might really be gone. Things like that just don't happen to us ordinary people, just to other people, you know, on TV, or something."

"I know what you mean. It's the first time anything like this has ever happened in our little town. You must have zoomed in for this picture."

"Yes."

"I like the way it's framed with Butt Butte in the background."

Jonah and Annie were both enjoying the performance Letty was giving for the children as he showed her the rest of his pictures. "Did you see Penn while you were picnicking?"

"I saw his pickup. It makes me shiver all over to think that girl was there when we were there."

"I wonder why she didn't see you and holler at you."

Annie turned and looked away from him.

He continued. "Dickie said she told him that you killed Penn and that you were going to kill her too."

"What! Are you serious? That's the most outrageous thing I've ever heard. Why in the world would she?"

"Yes, she told him, 'The old ladies did it and they're after me too.'"

"I must talk to Oliver, this is really unsettling, oh, there he is, right over there. Oliver! Oliver!" Annie waved as she and Jonah Souser started toward Oliver who had just parked near the fountain to watch the festivities.

"Hello Annie, Professor Souser, fine day, professor! What happened to you? Have you been in a fight?"

"Actually, yes. I was fighting with my suspenders."

"It must have been quite a fight?"

"Yes it was," the professor seemed preoccupied. "Might I add the suspenders won!"

"Jonah tells me that Angela is accusing Letty and I of some pretty terrible things. Is this really true?"

"She's still hysterical, I think. The doctor said being up there by herself for so long really got to her. I guess she's afraid of being alone anyway. She's been talking about wild animals and ghosts, and all sorts of things. He's hoping therapy will help. At this point, she doesn't seem to recognize reality."

"Poor child. Is she going to be alright?"

"They don't know yet."

"Her grandfather must be devastated."

"Yes, I was told he blames Penn."

"Are you any closer to finding Penn?" asked the Professor.

"No, nothing new, I'm sorry."

"I was just telling Annie, things like this just don't happen to us, they happen to someone else."

"Yes, we all have this mind set, like bad things only happen to people who deserve them, so when bad things happen to good people, it's hard to accept."

"Oliver, look at Jonah's picture. Isn't it beautiful?"

"Yes it is, it really is. Is this another prize winning entry?"

"I don't know yet, I just developed it this morning. I'll take it home and spend a few days looking at it before I decide."

"I think you have another winner," said Annie. "I love the colors. It must be a sunrise."

"Yes, it is."

Letty was still dancing on the pool wall. Charity watched her with a fascinated interest. The old lady moved so gracefully. She made it look so easy. How easy it was to admire her. After a while Letty came over to where Charity was standing, "Charity do you like my dancing?"

"You dance beautifully."

"Charity, you've always been too good to me. You're so sweet."

"Letty, you're a very special friend." *I need to talk to Letty. Maybe she has information she's not sharing—maybe she knows more than she's telling—maybe Penn's still alive, somehow, no, I know better than that. I just want him to still*

125

be alive. Everything is going to be so different. "I hope you feel the same way."

"Why yes, of course I do."

"Is there anything you can think of about Penn that you haven't already told someone? You know, something he might have said to you, something important?"

"He said he loved me. He played the piano for me. He said he loved to watch me dance. So I danced and I danced. I love to dance for Penn."

Oliver had been eavesdropping, unintentionally, of course. "Letty, how did Professor Souser get those bruises, do you know?"

"He fell in, then his six pack went in right after. He couldn't get into the boat. All that fighting to get in, overturned the boat. It was terrible, he was all wet. I had to close my eyes. My Papa went on a white water expedition. Did I ever tell you about that, hey Oliver?"

"No . . . ah, Letty, could we talk about the professor's bruises?"

"Papa and Lord Mountbatten were floating down the Colorado River— "

"Letty, not now."

"Their guides were arguing. It turned into a real brawl and they overturned the boat. Papa and Lord Mountbatten almost drowned . . . almost buried alive under all that water, like him, except he was by himself."

Oliver stood shaking his head— *This is getting me nowhere . . . again!*

CHAPTER 13

Boys and Their Toys

Rainbow's End was another road that ran along the lake before disappearing behind the Butte, or Butt Butte, as it was commonly called. Souser lived on Rainbow's End, three houses up from the lake, which could be seen easily from his front windows. The light green house was clearly a step above the surrounding houses. It had a spacious look to it with little shrubbery around, but a well manicured rose garden off to one side. To the other side, a grape arbor and patio finished framing the house as if it were all a part of a picture. It had a clean, well cared for look, yet denounced a woman's touch. There was no sign of life, as Oliver rang the bell several times, until finally, his hair mussed and sleepy-eyed, the professor answered— "Yes?"

"Professor Souser, were you napping?" He paused, thinking he heard a grunt from the professor, then continued, "May I come in?"

Oliver winched at the sight of his face as the professor opened the door wider to admit him. If anything it had gotten worse. "What did you say happened to you?" Oliver was trying to be polite.

"Do I have to tell you?"

"I think so— " Oliver said seriously.

"I was fishing down by the rapids and fell in. Annie and

Letty— "

"Enough said!" Oliver couldn't hold back his amusement. He burst out laughing.

"Might I suggest, out of courtesy, you could try to contain that?"

"I'm sorry! Continue, please."

"I slipped and my hip boots filled with water. I was fighting the current and my suspenders at the same time. My suspenders won. When I finally got the snaps to work, they sprang loose and came back and caught me full in the face. If Annie and Letty hadn't shown up at the exact moment they did in that rubber raft I wouldn't be here right now. I'd be somewhere in the wild blue yonder, sitting front row center with my two deceased friends."

"Freudian slip, professor?"

"Huh?"

"Deceased friends?"

"Wouldn't common sense kick in here? I mean, they probably are dead, aren't they?"

"We can't assume anything. Do you know something I don't?"

"No, of course not. I heard on the news this morning and then Katherine called. Do you really think there's foul play involved?"

"I don't know, Professor, I was hoping you could shed some light on the matter for me. Does O'Coins ever just go off like this?"

"Well, maybe, but he wouldn't right now, he has a summer job. They haven't seen him either."

"Any guesses?"

Souser bit into his lower lip with a frown, before continuing, "Perhaps you should talk to Letty—"

"Is the relationship they're having a serious one, do you know?"

"I didn't think so for a long time, but here just recently, I don't know, his attitude toward her seemed to have changed lately."

"What about Classie Acts?"

"Oh boy! He's going to get himself into hot water over that one if he doesn't watch out."

"Is there really anything going on between them?"

"I shouldn't tell on him, but there is, and he's going to get himself fired if her grandfather doesn't do him in first."

"I understand there was a big party last night at the Bearzall Estate. Didn't the news of O'Coins disappearance dampen your spirits just a little?"

"Yes, I think everyone drank a little heavy last night, except for Katherine, she didn't drink at all. Maybe she was worried about Penn— "

"If she was worried. Why didn't she drink too?"

"Katherine doesn't drink when she's upset or worried, keeps her head clear."

"Would she have reason to be more worried than anyone else?"

"It's just a rumor, we're all good friends, leave it at that!"

"Charity said you and Professor Bearzall left together. Tell me about that."

"Yes we wandered down to the boat dock. He wanted me to get in that row boat with him. I was snookered, but not that snookered. When he started the Elizabethan jargon, I left."

"What kind of jargon did you say?"

"Elizabethan, when he gets plowed, he thinks he's Shakespeare incarnate."

"Oh, okay. Where did you go then?"

"I went home."

"Did you see anyone?"

"No. Hey, wait a minute! Letty saw me from her window. She was out there on her balcony dancing for O'Coins again."

"She knows he's disappeared, why would . . . no, I'm not even going to ask that one. Have the police been here yet?"

"No. They were at Penn's this morning. I heard voices. They were swarming all over the place."

"Where does he live?"

"Right behind me here," he pointed to the house one up from his.

"Do you think it would be okay if I went up there for a look around?"

"I don't see why not. Come on, I'll walk with you." The two were silent as they walked. O'Coins' house was similar to Souser's, only a little smaller and with a large carport. The yard was somewhat unkept. Rhododendrons brightened the front of the house and the shutters and border work added even more color. There was a garden hose still laying in the overgrown grass. As they reached the front of the house, Oliver turned to look out across the valley floor.

"Wow, what a view!"

"I have basically, the same view from my place."

"Yes, the Tower's Estate can be easily seen from here. Which window is Letty's?"

"On the second floor. See the balcony, just right of the main entrance?"

"Is that where she dances at night?"

"Yes."

Oliver and Jonah poked around Penn's house for a while before returning to Jonah's.

"Come on in Oliver. I'll make us some iced coffee and try to remember if Letty was dancing the night Penn disappeared. I know she was last night."

"Maybe you could humor my curiosity. O'Coins took a great deal of pride in that old pickup of his, didn't he?"

"That's an understatement. That old truck glowed in the dark, it was so shinny. He spent a lot of time tinkering with it. Every time it burped, he put more money into it."

"It doesn't sound like you approve."

"It's his beast, mine's photography. To each his own. Oh, could you hand me those photos, the ones you're almost sitting on. I shouldn't have left them laying there. I've been looking all over for them. Funny, I seem to be getting more forgetful all the time. Thank you."

"Oh say, this is a good picture of O'Coins and Miss Letty."

"Yes it is. Good shot of his Jimmy too."

"I wonder what he's saying to her? Did you hear any of that conversation?"

"No, I didn't. She's probably telling him another one of her stories."

"Not the way he's looking at her, really absorbed in their conversation, it looks like he's saying something and she's listening, intently."

"You're right, I'd never really noticed before. He wanted a picture of the Jimmy. It was Letty's idea for the both of them to be in the picture."

"This was just taken, wasn't it?"

"Yes, just a couple of days before graduation, as a matter of fact. Penn and I had just returned from lunch and he asked me to shoot his pickup before it got dusty. He had just waxed it, anyway, Letty happened by at exactly that moment. She grabbed Penn by the arm and pulled him in front of the rig and I took the picture. I've been laughing about it ever since."

"I understand some of your photos are pretty good?"

"Would you like to see some of my best efforts?"

"I'd love to. Wait a minute! Why would Letty be dancing for O'Coins if he's missing?"

"Ah, might I suggest she's flipped out completely?"

"Okay. I said I was going to stay away from that one, didn't I?"

Jonah Souser led Oliver into his den where the walls were lined with photos. "Some are old and some are new. I've been at this for quite a while."

"Boy, I guess you have. This one here . . . "

"The Buick La Sabra, yes, one of my favorites. That car traveled a lot of miles with me. This was taken a number of years ago, at the fair. The carnival in the background and all the lights really set the car off, don't you think?"

"Sure does. You liked this car, huh?"

"Yes I did, why?"

"I have one just like it, except mine's icky brown."

"No kidding, is it an 87?"

"Yes."

"Well, I'll be. I'd like to see it if you don't mind?"

"She's sitting right outside— "

Like two schoolboys, they went over every nick and chip. Oliver had a story for every one, which Jonah could match. Their car stories soon began to sound like fish stories. They carried their stories back inside and embellished some more over straight shots and chips. The sun began to sink behind the hill before Oliver realized he hadn't yet checked in with the Mad Hatter, but instead of going directly to his radio, he left Jonah's and parked below near Annie's favorite bench. He rolled down his window and sat listening to the night sounds.

Lights from the college and surrounding city blinked in the expanse. Duck Lake looked almost like a well-lighted football field. Shadows danced on the water as if they were gleefully laughing at a half baked detective— "We have secrets too deep for your grasping!" They seemed to be taunting him.

A wisp of air rustled the branches overhanging the water near-by. Oliver felt a shiver run the full length of his spine. It was as if something just a little bit spooky had just touched him. "Bunnie, are you there?"

"Yes Olie. Boy are you in hot water again."

"I've been sitting here by the lake. Somehow, I've got a real eerie feeling all of a sudden, like the water is hiding something from us."

"Well, you'd better connect with reality long enough to face the firing squad. I don't think you'll have to worry about it till morning though, she went home. That's where most sane people go after dark, you know, home?"

"Am I keeping you, Bunnie? Hey kid, go on home."

"Thank you. What about you?"

"I think I'll just sit here awhile. Night Bunnie."

"Night Olie."

Wrapped snugly in his blankets, Oliver woke with a start to Bunnie's voice. His radio was singing wildly— "Oliver, do you copy? Come in, Oliver, Olie! This is important! You'd better put your ears on."

"Okay Bunnie, I'm here. What's going on?" Oliver was brushing the sleep out of his eyes as he turned to look at the clock.

"You'd better get your butt in gear and get into the office. The Mad Hatter just came in and you're late. Are you even out of bed yet?"

"Never made it to bed, I slept in the car." Oliver had been suffering from feelings of inferiority for several days now and was in no mood to be confronted by the Mad Hatter, so when he arrived, he tried to tip-toe past her door.

"Oliver, is that you?"

"Yes, it is." He stopped and made an about-face, hesitant, at first.

"Come in here, please?"

A look of surprise spread across Oliver's face as he entered the small cubby-hole his boss called her office. "You're not mad at me?"

"My therapist says I need to learn how to be nicer to people, so I'm trying to be nice to everyone for a whole day, okay?"

"Sure. Does that mean I'm really going to get it tomorrow?"

The look she shot across to him could have been mistaken for an evil eye. "Let's get on with today," she said. "I've been looking over your case here. Let me see, we have two professors missing. No clues, no real motives! Any ideas? Come on, throw some ideas at me and I'll cut them down. In the process, maybe we'll stumble upon something that makes sense."

"Maybe Bearzall bumped O'Coins off to get rid of his competition. Bearzall needs to feed his ego. O'Coins knew Classie was playing him for a fool for the grade. He didn't care, but Bearzall needs the conquest for his self esteem. Jealousy could be a motive."

"But we don't know that he's dead and Bearzall hasn't been gone long enough to even call it a 'missing persons' yet."

"The guy was drunk. He was in a row boat, out on the lake all alone— "

"Did anyone actually see him get into that boat after Souser left?"

"No, I don't think so, unless . . . perhaps Letty saw something, but you never know with her. She can't remember what's real and what's imaginary, I don't think. At least, if she does, she's not going to let on."

"Maybe, maybe we'd better drag the lake."

"I can set that up."

"Letty, we're getting lazy."

"What do you mean?"

"We sit here in front of the coffee shop day after day admiring the waterfall. How long has it been since we actually went to the waterfall?"

"You mean the one up on the mountain?"

"Yes, the real one."

"We can pack a lunch and have a picnic— "

"A picnic is what got us into trouble the first time."

"We won't be seeing anyone at the falls, besides, Penn's not running loose anymore. I think a lunch will be super. Let me see, cold chicken, fried just a little too much and strawberry daiquiris."

"What?"

"Well, that's what they say in the movies— "

"No, 'Penn's not running loose anymore,' what do you mean by that?"

"Oh, do you remember those horrible, horrible movies, the mummies always dug their way out of the graves and then had secret hiding places, a strawberry daiquiri in hand. And they always laughed a hideous laugh. Maybe we should take Jezebel with us, for protection, you know. I haven't tried strawberry daiquiris, maybe Jezebel would like that? She's getting pickier and pickier."

"How are we supposed to take Jezebel? Is she going to get up and walk?"

"Oh, I forgot she's getting so big. We can't carry her anymore can we? And she's getting weak besides."

"She's too weak to walk by herself?"

"You're making fun of me now. You'd be surprised what she could do if she was eating right. I don't understand. She won't eat anything I like. I cook everything just exactly the way I like it and she won't eat it."

"Maybe she wants her dinner to dance for her?"

"What did you say? Never mind—let's go!"

The ladies walked home and hurriedly threw together some things to swim in and piled into Matilda for an afternoon of fun.

"Oh Annie, look! We're part of the parade."

"I forgot about Graffiti Night. Wouldn't you know!"

"Smile nice and wave Annie. Do we have any candy? Look at that Model A pickup. I wonder if that's the original paint job?"

"Florescent orange?"

"Oh look! A thirty-seven Ford, just like Papa used to have."

"A cut-down stock car. It's been a long time since I've seen one of those. How do we get out of this mess?"

"Here Annie, turn quick!"

"All this to go pick up picnic supplies."

"You wait here while I go in and get our supplies. We can pretend we're on a safari and have to combat lions to get to higher ground. Oh, this is so exciting. I won't be too long, Sis, we want to swim before the sun goes down."

Annie sat, watching children running through the sprinkler on the college grounds adjacent to the super market.

"Hello."

"Jonah, hello yourself. I thought you'd be fishing."

"After the other day's adventure, perhaps it's best if I just take it easy today. What about you?"

"We're headed for the falls for a picnic and swim, your shiner looks as bad as it did yesterday—"

"I guess I need a good nurse."

"I can't stand to see you in pain."

Jonah started to reach for Annie's arm resting on the open window of her car door, when— "

"Professor," interrupted Letty, "Ouch, that has to be painful."

"Hello, Letty. Not unless I laugh. Here, let me help you with that sack."

"Would you like to go swimming with us at the falls?"

"Oh, no, thank you. I've had enough of your fresh water recreation to last me for a while."

"Well, Annie and I are going swimming at the falls. We're taking a picnic lunch with us too."

"Yes, it looks good— well, I'll see you ladies another time."

The ladies left town and started up the mountain.

135

"Do you ever daydream Annie? I mean about Jonah? You know—"

"Daydream? It wouldn't do me any good. He's always thinking about intellectual things or fishing—"

"But, what do you daydream about?"

Annie pushed the accelerator down and squealed rubber around the graveled turns.

"Swimming and picnicking in the sunshine," she said. She shot a smile sideways at her little sister.

"How sad," answered Letty, "I daydream about men all the time," and with that, was lost in her own thoughts the rest of the way.

"Are we here? It looks just like it did when we were girls. Oh what memories I have of this place."

"Did Bartrum ever bring you up here?"

"Letty Tower, that's quite enough! Bartrum didn't take me anyplace. Papa wouldn't let me go with him."

Letty snickered as she ran off ahead of Annie, making sure she was out of reach and then laughed out loud. Then, calling over her shoulder she asked, "Will our picnic things be okay here? Can we swim first?"

"Okay, it's going to taste so good after a nice cool swim. I can smell the water, can't you?"

"I can smell the chicken. It makes my mouth water. Oh no! I forgot the olives."

"That's okay. It's going to taste good anyway. Let's go jump in. I wonder if the cave is still the way it used to be?"

"Let's go see."

"Last one across is the rotten egg."

"That's not fair. I'm always the rotten egg."

They plunged in together and swam the thirty feet to the other side. The ferns had grown larger and finding footholds and handholds became most important.

"Follow the ledge. Okay, now feel for the one under your feet. Follow it around. That's right, now through the falls . . . wow!"

"Annie, I'd forgotten how beautiful this is—"

"And I'd forgotten about all the slimy moss and bugs—"

"Look at Matilda, sitting over there all forlorn, she can't see us. Do you think she's wondering what happened to us?"

"Let's start back."

They made their way back through the falls and swam across.

"How are we going to dry off? Matilda won't like us climbing in wet."

"Remember how we used to take sunbaths?

"Yes, after we eat, we can take a sunbath. We can lay here in the grass and get a tan."

"We'll more likely freckle—"

"Come on, Annie, live dangerously for once."

"I went rafting with you, wasn't that dangerous enough? What about pushing your true love into a hole? Huh?"

"Let's try for a different kind of dangerous. You know, have you ever needed help finding your own bedroom?"

"No, have you?"

"No, but I have tip-toed up the stairs a few times."

"Letty, what am I to do with you? You brought booze again."

"Oh Annie, you're a party pooper. Come on, let's have a happy drink and get warm and fuzzy before we eat."

"Then we're sure to have nightmares tonight."

"Nice warm, fuzzy, cuddly nightmares. Oh, yes— "

CHAPTER 14

A Peaceful Exchange

Oliver and Madelynn were both in the office and it was after 9:00 PM. Bunnie was still there wrapping up as well. The three of them together after hours was extremely unusual, maybe even a first. Madelynn put her sharp edge away and Oliver sat with his feet propped on his desk. Bunnie sensed the welcome atmosphere and lingered.

Madelynn sat at her desk with head propped on one hand laughing in amusement. "That loony old lady and her frogs."

"And bubbles, don't forget the bubbles," Oliver chimed in.

"Did I ever tell you my dad was a frogman in the Navy?" Bunnie looked first at Oliver, then Madelynn. The laughter stopped. Oliver sprung to his feet and threw his hands wildly over his head. Madelynn looked like she'd seen a ghost.

"What did I say?"

"That's it! Letty's been telling us all along. That loony old lady. She's been telling us all along and we haven't been listening." Oliver brushed his hand through his hair excitedly before sitting down again.

"You know . . . this is bigger than just two little old ladies' infatuation gone array. This sounds more like organized crime. Oliver, I want you to check the wire on a regular bases . . . look for anything unusual, you know . . . anything that's bigger than just local stuff. Especially if there's an unsolved murder floating around, something like that."

"We don't have much time. The District Attorney is jumping on the band wagon. He's demanding a speedy trial; says that he can convict the old ladies."

"And of course, he's going to try to tie the two disappearances together. After Angela pointed her finger at them, it doesn't look good."

"I've been poking around . . ." Oliver hesitated.

"I'm listening."

"I've got some strange information recently that might be related— I guess I better check the wires back a ways, maybe even back to when the festival was going on."

Madelynn sat forward and the atmosphere changed abruptly. "What would make you think— you've been withholding information from me!"

"No— no, it might not have anything to do with it. This thing just keeps getting weirder and weirder. It might even tie in with the stolen bicycles. You've got to admit, Tower Falls never has any crime."

"You're right, no crime. Now, how would bicycles tie into this?" Madelynn paused as Bunnie reentered the room with fresh coffee.

"Looks like it's going to be a long night."

"Hey, Bunnie! What do you know about bicycles?"

Bunnie looked startled. "What about bikes? I was only a little kid. Really, when that happened. I wouldn't have been caught if it hadn't flipped on me. I had three stitches over that and a juvenile record."

"What are we talking about? Oliver, do you know what she's talking about?"

Oliver's face was a puzzle.

"Aren't you referring to my juvenile record for bike stealing?"

Oliver and Madelynn looked from one to another, then Oliver asked, "Why did you steal a bike?"

"Does it matter?"

"Just out of curiosity, okay?"

Bunnie sighed. "I stole the bike to create a diversion for my cousin while he copped a pack of cigarettes."

"You what?" Maadelyn suddenly zeroed in.

140

"I was only seven."

"That's it— twenty-seven bicycles in one week. Where were we headed just prior to that? Thanks, Bunnie. Score two for Bunnie."

"So you think our stolen bicycles are a diversion?"

"Big possibility. I might have something else you'll be interested in as well. The night Annie went with Souser, O'Coins wined and dined Letty. Want more?"

"Go on."

"They were seen by Professor Bearzall and his wife, the bartender at the Buzzard's Branch, and numerous witnesses."

"Who would ever think Mr. 'Full of Himself' would be having an affair with a dotty old lady! So, what else have you got?"

"You look like the cat that swallowed the rat, what have you got?"

"Just this," she said with a crooked smile and squinted eyes. "They found O'Coins pickup early this morning in the lake, along with Bearzall's watch and sweater not ten feet from it. What do you make of that?"

"So my eerie feelings at the lake last night were right. Ten to one, they'll find Bearzall in the lake too. Are they going to be able to pull any finger prints from the truck?"

"Probably not, it was embedded in slime, this is Duck Lake we're talking about, get real! They said they'd try though."

"I don't know why I'm here. Why am I humoring you? You're going to get us both in more trouble than we can handle." Annie shuffled her feet uneasily, looking over her shoulder to the building behind them.

"I need to see the pickup. I need to assess the damage and find the little black box."

"An airplane has a little black box, Letty, not a pickup."

"This one has a little black box. Trust me. It's under the driver's seat."

"Your running record tells me not to, anyway. How are we going to get to it?"

"We'll go over and talk to the nice men trying to clean it out and we can offer to help clean it."

"I don't think that'll work. They're not exactly cleaning it. They're looking for evidence too. I doubt they'll let us near it."

"We don't know that, do we?"

"Have you thought this through?"

"Yes, see, I even brought my school bag. You go be nice to the man over there while I slip over to the door on the driver's side and sneak the box into my bag."

"I can't believe I'm consenting to be a part of your craziness."

"I love you too, Sissy."

The ladies followed through with Letty's plan without a hitch and soon were on their way home. As they pulled into their driveway, they found Oliver there, waiting for them. He purposely looked past them and addressed their car.

"Hello Matilda," he said, with a troubled frown.

"Oliver, do you have any more news? Has anything else happened?"

"Yes, as a matter of fact," Oliver paused and pursed his lips for a moment before he continued. "We found what was left of a six-pack of Hamm's and O'Coins pickup this morning. You hadn't heard yet?"

"No . . . oh, no . . . what next?" *Everything is beginning to snowball.*

"Are you alright, Annie?" Letty was watching her sister intently.

"We figure," continued Oliver, noticing that Annie had turned white, "That Classie's grandfather did away with O'Coins. He must be dead."

"He's not dead," said Letty, "We thought he was. We even buried him, but the crack kept getting bigger."

Oliver raised both eyebrows and cast a knowing look in Annie's direction. *Here we go again! Poor Annie, I'd turn white too.*

While Oliver was helping unload some groceries, Annie turned to Letty, "How dare you, I can't turn my back on you!"

Letty bristled suddenly, "I can tell when I'm not wanted," and holding her school bag tight to her, disappeared into the house.

"Those crazy old ladies were here poking around. The one with the curls, she was over there and I'm sure I saw her slip something into her bag, but when I asked, she didn't seem to know how to answer my questions. She was telling me about her nanny, something about a nanny who stole the Imperial Emeralds and consequently was eaten by a Bengal tiger."

"Oh yes, I'm familiar with her story telling."

It had been unseasonably warm the past few days. "The Snoop Shop," even with both fans on, was beginning to feel like a locker room. Earlier Oliver and Madelynn had pulled the partitions out between the desks to allow a freer air flow and he could easily hear her rummaging through papers behind him, but he chose to ignore her little noises. Rubbing his head, "We've found Classie, and O'Coins' pickup, but where in tarnation is O'Coins? Everywhere I turn leads to a dead end that has a crack in it. Those crazy old ladies and their crack!"

"Their what?" Madelynn peered up at him over the rim of her reading glasses. She seemed more interested in her paperwork than in his proclamation.

"Oh my gosh! Maybe they did do him in. Those two smart, daffy, old ladies! That's it! I know where he is!" He jumped up, hollering Indian war dance fashion— "Get backup . . . a search warrant too! Follow me out to the Tower Estate."

"This better be good!"

"He's under the hot tub Madelynn. I know it! I know he is! That's why it's got a crack in it."

CHAPTER 15

The Mad Hatter

Tower Fall's Chief of Detectives, Madelynn Hatter pulled up in front of the large estate to find Oliver waiting patiently for her on the front steps. During his wait, he had gone over every piece of information they had up to this point, jotting down the pieces of the puzzle until all the pieces formed a perfect picture. Madelynn stepped from the car and turned to face Oliver. He stood with his finger to his mouth.

"Shhhhhh," he whispered. "The ladies haven't spotted me yet."

"Oliver," she whispered. "What are we doing here? I ordered a digging crew at your request and a search warrant . . . this better be good or you'll get hung out to dry."

With a search warrant in hand, the digging in Planet Venus began. After Madelynn phoned for a search warrant, she'd called for reinforcement from Centerville. It had fallen together so nicely, right down to every minute detail. The two old ladies had, indeed, buried O'Coins under the hot tub. Oliver shuddered when he thought of the times he had splashed and enjoyed the merrymaking in that very tub.

Annie stood watching the digging wringing her hands in agony. *They're going to find him and haul me away and Letty can't take care of herself. What ever am I to do?*

"Annie! Where's your manners? I've not forgotten mine." Letty poured several glasses of iced lemonade, "here you go. Have some nice refreshments."

The digging crew, Centerville's Special Unit, and Madelynn chorused a hearty "thank you", while Oliver swallowed hard and whispered a "no thank you," to Letty.

Morning turned into afternoon and finally, the hot tub was removed from its place in the Planet Venus.

As Oliver S. Homes and Madelynn Hatter stood looking on, the special unit from Centerville stirred around in the loose earth in the bottom of the reopened hole. Oliver stood, his feet planted apart and arms folded with a smug look on his face. He knew he had cracked this case. He knew the body was there. He could read Annie's face and knew she knew the body was there, too. Letty was now nowhere to be seen and he wondered about that, but the soon to be glory drew his attention back to the digging in the bottom of the hole, and then, "There ain't nothing here, folks. Who's hair-brained idea was this, anyway?"

Oliver's hand and mouth dropped at the same time. "Annie, are you alright?" He had regained his composure enough to be concerned for Annie who turned very pale and slowly sunk to the floor. She lay completely still, partially hidden by the tropical foliage. The first one to her, Oliver lifted her limp head and patted her on the check. Finally, she began to stir.

"I feel rather shaky, a little weak." *Oh my, oh my, she dug him up, what did she do with him, oh no, she stuffed him.* "I think I'm going to be ill."

"Here, let me help you up." Madelynn and Oliver took her into the parlor and helped her to a chair.

"Do you have anything in the house I can get for you to drink?"

"Letty has— " As she turned to Oliver, "Oliver, have you seen Letty?"

"No, I don't remember seeing her after she served lemonade a few hours ago. Oh, don't tell me. Annie, when was the last time you saw her?"

"Not since lemonade either."

Madelynn turned to Oliver— "Oh, that's just great! What do we have, another missing person? Oliver, you've a lot to answer for. I hope you know your hide's on the line this time. I'm going to enjoy making you history."

"Just a minute. Annie, we need to start looking for Letty, right now."

At that precise moment, Letty came walking down the marble staircase, stretching sleepily as if she had just been awakened. "I was having such a nice dream. It was about Wee Willy. He has a nice smile, don't you think, Annie? What are all these people doing here? Annie, where are your manners? Have you offered these nice people some lemonade?"

They all shivered.

Madelynn and Oliver stood silently, looking into the empty pit that had held the hot tub. Oliver was waiting to be yelled at.

"Oliver, what's the shinny object next to that pipe?" She was pointing toward the lead-in pipe. Oliver slid down into the dirt hole to investigate. "Look at what I found. You don't suppose this watch belongs to someone we know, do you?"

"What is this, the revenge of the watches? Let me see it." Madelynn turned the watch over and wiped the back. "There's writing here. Okay, it says— "To my Beloved from Letty.' Who do you suppose her Beloved is?"

"I know who her Beloved is, Penny O'Coins. Now, what do we do?"

"Okay, we know he was here before the hot tub was installed. Get your records and find out when he disappeared."

"I know when he disappeared. He was here the night he disappeared. I'll check the records to find out when the hot tub was installed. If I remember right Mrs. Dustvaffor said there was some weird goings-on the day after O'Coins disappeared."

"What are you standing here for? Move it!"

"Yes Sir!"

Oliver stopped by the café in the square to pick up a

mocha and then decided to sit at a table in front to drink it. Before he knew it, he was in the phone booth dialing Barbie's number.

"Hello?"

"Hello, Barbie?"

"Yes, who is this?"

"This is Oliver, I—"

"How'd you get my number?"

"Ah . . . Bunnie gave it to me. You aren't angry are you?"

"Bunnie's my best friend. I guess it's okay, she wouldn't give it to just anyone."

"She's like a best friend to me too. She's saved my neck more than once or twice, anyway, what I'm calling about is there any chance you would consider going out with me? I'd really like to see you."

"I thought you'd never ask."

"A nice candle-light dinner, we could go to, oh, I got a better idea: a river boat cruise, yes! Do you get sea-sick?"

"What?"

"I mean, I can get tickets for dinner on a cruise ship up the river— "

"A cruise? How long is this date going to last?"

"Oh, just a few hours, I'd have you back by daylight."

"Daylight? When are you picking me up?"

"You mean that's a yes?"

There was a pause on the other end of the line, then, "Yes, I'd love to. When are you picking me up?"

"We have to be on board by sunset."

"About 8:00, then?"

"I should probably pick you up by, at least 7:00. The boat leaves at sunset."

"Dinner on a cruise ship. This is heavy for a first date."

"Not really. We'll never be alone. There's dinner, and entertainment. It's a dinner theater."

"What's a dinner theater?"

"That's where you eat and watch a play at the same time."

"Do you know what the play is going to be?"

"No, I do know it will be a mystery— "

"Like a detective story?"

"Yes. We can even be part of the play, if we want."

"Sounds like fun and you sound like fun. When are we going to do this?"

"How about Friday night? Are you free Friday night?"

"I can be. I have time coming."

"Great! I'll see you at 7:00 Friday night."

"I'll be looking forward to this— "

"Yes, me too." *Yes! Yes! Yes! Wow! Just look at her . . . that's the sexiest dress I've ever seen. Oh, low cut in the back. All the men are staring at her and wishing they were me.*

"Buster, I've been banging on this phone booth for ten minutes. What the heck are you doing, anyway?"

"Oh, sorry, yes of course. Here you go." Oliver was red faced as he left the booth and headed for his car.

"Oliver, where are you?" His radio crackled, "I've been trying to reach you. Dang-it, Oliver, put your ears on and listen up!"

"Ah, yeah. Bunnie, I hear you, okay?"

"It's about time. The hatter's at it again."

"What's her problem this time?"

"Let's just say, she's a little reluctant to do any more digging— "

"That's too bad. I love to dig in the dirt, play in the mud, even."

"This last bit, the hot tub? Well, it has her steaming, no pun intended, what do you mean, play in the mud, Oliver, you're strange."

"Yeah, I know, okay, I'm on my way."

"Have you checked your records yet?"

"Yes and I have an idea."

"Well, what? Are you waiting for Sherlock Holmes to tell you what to do?"

Oliver took a deep breath and slowly began to unravel his deductions. "O'Coins was messing around with Goldsworth's granddaughter. He had been seen threatening O'Coins and he had a gun. We know O'Coins was buried in the hot tub hole because we found his watch there. The old boy killed O'Coins and buried him there before the hot tub was installed and— "

149

"Whoa, wait a minute! We found his watch, that doesn't mean he was buried there, and besides, how did Goldsworth know there was a hot tub going in there?"

"Everyone knew it was well advertised. So where better to bury a dead body than in an already dug hole?"

"Okay, so where's the body? Any idea?"

"You're going to think this is crazy, but Letty and Annie dug him up and hid him in that big old house somewhere."

"How would they have known he was there?"

"In my notes, Letty spoke about being up all night, supposedly polishing silver. She said she had to get the silver polished before daylight because Annie would be getting back then."

"What does polishing silver have to do with anything?"

"No, no, that was her excuse for being up all night. They must have caught Goldsworth and they were digging him up. Those two old ladies buried him someplace else. Either that or they threw him in the lake."

"Why would they do that?"

"You don't know those two old ladies, do you?"

"I don't think your theory will hold water. Even though everyone knew about the hot tub, how would he get in without being seen? The ladies keep everything locked up tight. Besides, that old man couldn't haul around 180 pounds of dead weight by himself."

"Well, maybe someone helped him. Maybe that's how the old ladies knew where the body was. Maybe they helped him."

"You're grabbing at straws, Oliver."

"Okay then, here's another straw. Professor Souser was taking pictures up by the tower. I got the impression he was up there the same day the ladies were picnicking. That didn't come out until he showed Annie a picture he took. Why didn't he say something about being up there before this? He was the last one to see Bearzall alive too. We mustn't lose sight of that either."

"Motive, Oliver, we need a motive."

"Okay, I've got two motives for you. First, who would be President of the college if Bearzall were gone? Penny O'Coins is next in line, but now he's gone too. So that leaves our dear

Professor Souser, home free as President. He's not getting any younger, you know. Secondly, we have rumors that can be substantiated that Bearzall and O'Coins were both fooling around with Angela to fix her grades. Souser would never ever allow that. He's too self-righteous, he did it to keep the school's name unblemished."

"These might be valid motives, but you're still doing a lot of fancy footwork. Try giving me evidence, you know, proof positive."

"Bearzall and Souser were at the lake together. Souser saw Letty on her balcony that night. She may have seen what happened."

"Keep going— "

"I saw Professor Souser earlier today. He's battered and bruised, with the biggest shiner I've ever seen. Supposedly a fishing accident."

"Go on— "

"I talked to Letty, too. She said he couldn't get into the boat because of the fight. She even mentioned an overturned boat. She might be in danger. If Souser was sure she saw and was able to put it all together, she would be a threat to him. She might even know what happened to O'Coins."

"I want to see those pictures you were talking about. The ones Souser took the day O'Coins disappeared."

"I'll need a search warrant."

"You've got it. I'll call the Judge. When we get the warrant, I want to be there for the search. However Mr. Homes, I am a reluctant player. You've already been wrong on this case. I don't want a repeat! "

"Madelynn, over here— "

"What have you got?"

"A note. Look, he keeps his personal notes . . . look at this one."

"Let me see— 'Mind your own business, Jonah. Your opinion carries no weight. What I do with my students is none of your business. Dickie.'"

"That's good. Now have you found any pictures?"

"No. They're probably at school. He takes his pictures in to

151

the dark room in the Photography lab at school. Why didn't I think of that?"

"You'll need a separate search warrant for that."

"I know."

"And if you're wrong. You're going to have the whole college down on us."

"I'm not wrong."

"You'd better not be."

Annie was in her room laying flat on her back in bed. She'd heard that would keep her blood pressure down and she didn't want to have any more fainting spells. She turned slightly when she heard Letty tip-toeing in—

"Annie, I'm so sorry. I have a secret and I've been afraid to share it with you.

"Let me guess , you have him, you dug him up!"

"Yes, I have him in my secret room. Isn't that nice? Aren't you excited?"

Really in shock, Annie stared wide-eyed at Letty, and for once, at a loss for words. "He loves the secret room. He even watches out his window. He said his bed is comfy. Annie, are you listening to me?"

"Let me catch my breath. Okay Letty, did you stuff him?"

"Why of course, he said the food was delicious."

"Letty, come over here and sit down beside me and start from the beginning and tell me all about it."

"Okay, he just had a bump on his head, but it's okay, he's not angry with us, he got over being buried alive because he got out, that's what caused the crack."

"You mean to tell me, he's really alive? He's really here? Letty, why is he still here?"

"Annie, you don't understand. Classy's grandfather's going to kill him."

"Letty, I have to see him for myself. I find this really hard to believe."

"Annie, he is a little upset about his pickup. Promise you won't mention it, okay?"

"So where are you keeping him?"

"In the secret room behind my closet. You have one too,

152

remember? We used to play there when we were children, remember? Come on— "

"Art thou remembering my hunger, my True Love?"

"Shhhhh," Letty motioned to Annie, "He doesn't know you're with me. Penn, I'm not alone today. I brought Annie with me— "

The professor jumped to his feet and sucked in his breath as he straightened up— "Annie, now don't be angry. We can talk this through. I don't want you kicking at me again— "

"Sit down!" She stood for a moment looking at him and then her face softened. "Now that I can see you really are living and breathing, I think I had better call Oliver. That poor man is trying to solve the mystery of your death, maybe even nail Professor Souser for your untimely demise. I was about ready to give myself up. I knew he didn't do it and I couldn't look him in the eye. I've been worried sick about Letty. Whatever would she do if I were in Jail" Annie sat down too, rubbing her temples with both hands. "I think I need to take another Alky-Seltzer."

CHAPTER 16

Oliver's Induction

Oliver rose early in the morning, going over the ladies' chances in the hanging judge's courtroom as he shaved. "Thank god, it's only an inquest. Ouch!" Blood streamed down his chin. He reached for a tissue to stop the flow. "I need to stop off some time today and get new blades."

"The professor's been missing for too long. We all know he's dead. I know those two old ladies did it. I want to put Letty on the stand and make her confess. It doesn't make any difference if they are old, or rich, they're not exempt from the laws of this state."

Oliver could feel an anger beginning to boil within— the prosecutor seemed pleased that he had an open and shut case. "Your Honor, I've gotten to know these two old ladies over the past weeks. They're not capable of premeditation for murder or anything else, especially Letty. She doesn't operate on a full deck, bless her heart. Both ladies are special, they have more love to give than most."

"Are you saying they're incapable of understanding what they did?" The prosecutor chided belligerently.

"Whoa! Wait a minute! They didn't do anything. You have

to prove a crime was committed before you can even accuse them."

"I'm inclined to agree with the detective," said the judge. "Give me solid evidence that a crime was committed and enough evidence to convict them." Turning to Oliver, he continued, "Your ladies aren't off the hook, yet. There are a number of unanswered questions."

The door in the back of the court room slowly opened and the two ladies entered, tip-toeing to near-by seats. Their absence up to this point stood out like a sore thumb. The prosecutor watched them with furrowed brow as Letty adjusted and readjusted her purse, then stood up to take off her jacket. Her purse fell to the floor.

The bailiff came in and handed Oliver a note. As he read it, the color drained from his face. He sat slowly and with the most dumbfounded look, scanned the room for Madelynn. Spying her, he motioned and she came right over.

"What's going on?" she whispered.

He handed her the note and watched for a response—"Is there any way to cut into this proceeding? We've got to tell the judge."

Oliver stood up—"Your Honor, I have news the court will be interested in."

"Yes, Mr. Homes, speak up."

"Your Honor. If it pleases the court. I have a note here in my hand that states the professor has been found."

"Well, Mr. Homes, do speak up!"

"Your Honor, it seems Letty had him hidden in a secret room in the Tower's Estate. He's alive and well, Your Honor."

"Court's dismissed until this report can be checked out and verified. To be reconvened upon further notice. Mr. Homes, I'll see you in my chambers in fifteen minutes."

"Your Honor, I think if you talked with them, you would agree that there was no intent to commit a crime, unless being old and dotty is a crime. As hard as Letty tried to tell . . . her secret was the best kept one of all. O'Coins dug his way out from under the hot tub and hid himself in Letty's bedroom. The general consensus was that he must be dead.

156

They found his pickup in the lake and were sure that they would find his body there too. All this time, Letty's been hiding him in a secret room behind her closet. The room even has a window overlooking the lake where O'Coins has watched the events unfold. Letty finally went to Annie and told her what was going on, after the hot tub was dug up. Before then, she was sneaking food up to him. O'Coins wanted to hide because Angela's grandfather caught him in the super market parking lot and waved a pistol at him. He figured the old man really meant it and that he might just be crazy enough to use his pistol. He knew Letty would hide him so he went to her. He only meant to hide for a few days until Angela's grandfather had time to cool off, but then everything snowballed until he couldn't come out of hiding. Your Honor, I submit that these two ladies did nothing with intent to harm anyone. However, I have to admit," he added with a smile, "They did try to do me in, twice. First, with a lemonade that was so sour it would have done in a horse, and secondly, they served me a coffee so strong with whiskey, I nearly choked to death!"

"I see no case here, unless Mr. O'Coins wants to bring charges for what happened to his pickup. I don't see that happening. Let's go home. By the way, Mr. Homes, that tissue goes nicely with your shirt."

"Oh yes, Your Honor," reaching for his chin. He looked up in time to catch the judge smiling and his ears turned beet red.

The two ladies were waiting outside the judge's chamber and accompanied Oliver out of the building.

"Oh, what a glorious day. Oliver you know you're stuck with us now, don't you?"

"What do you mean, Annie?"

"You're part of the family now, young man."

"Oh dear, I don't know if I'm up to that, or not," he said, obviously enjoying all the attention.

"The next time we go to England, we're taking you with us," said Letty.

Oliver and Annie shot one another a glance as Letty

157

continued, "When Papa took us to England the first time, we found Camelot, where King Arthur held court. Excalaber, his sword was back in the stone where it belonged."

"Letty, that's not true— "

"It was back in the stone where it belonged."

"The legend says the sword was thrown back into the lake . . . to the maiden of the lake."

"I don't care what the legend says, the sword was back in the stone."

"It was not!"

"Was too!"

"Ladies, please!"

The two ladies looked at one another and burst out laughing. They locked arm and arm and continued on down the big steps. Letty stopped and turned to Annie with a frown. Then leaning toward her, she whispered, "Annie, what happened to Bearzall's beer?"

"Not another word." *I wonder what she is talking about, what beer?* "No story today, Letty." Annie sighed heavily.

"My family's full of nuts. We hatched, that's what Papa said—" Letty was giggling. "We all belong in the nut factory." Then she began singing— "I'm counting the nuts in my family tree, want to see who's closest to me. There's cousin Buryl, watch out for that squirrel. He moved too slow and now he's a girl." Oliver was watching for Annie's reaction so when he saw her laughing uncontrollably, he joined in. He was beginning to understand how the two old ladies stayed so young.

"Letty, have you worked in the nut hatchery all your life?" Oliver was beginning to feel like one of the family.

"You mean the booby-hatch, don't you?"

"Maybe. Letty, what were you telling Annie about Professor Bearzall?"

"That's a secret!"

"It's okay Letty, Oliver is one of the family now. We don't keep secrets from each other, remember?" Annie tried to coax Letty into a discussion.

"Professor Bearzall left with the frogs, remember? So, he

158

must have left."

"That sounds about right." Oliver tried not to show his disappointment.

"What about the frogs and bubbles?"

"I know that there will be more frogs, because it pulled him under. I never saw him come up. I wonder what it did with the beer? Frogs drink, I suppose, maybe I'll have a drink too."

Oliver shook his head in resignation. *We found the beer.*

"Yes, maybe a cup of tea will hit the spot."

"Tea? I need something stronger than tea. I still have some whiskey."

"Not this afternoon, dear, I'd better look at our calender. I know we have something to do this afternoon."

"We've got to go talk to the nice judge at the Court House. Can we dress up, Annie? Let's put on our Sunday best to meet her."

"We don't have to dress up dear, we're fine."

"Are you sure? I wouldn't want her to think we're poor."

"I don't think she will. I think she knows who we are. Go on ahead, dear, I forgot something. Oliver, could you help me, please?"

Letty left through the front door and they heard her singing as she promenaded across the lawn.

"Oliver," Annie tugged at his sleeve. "I'm concerned about Letty's new friend. I mean, I'm worried about Letty. I don't trust this man."

"Oh, the plant doctor's for real? I thought he was another story."

"No, he's been here several times for what he calls, 'plant therapy.' He says Jezebel is hostile toward men."

"He was here. . . in the house?"

"Every day this past week."

"I don't want you to get alarmed, Annie, but I want his name. I'm going to cheek this guy out."

"Dr. Theodore. Letty thinks he's Teddy reincarnated."

"This meeting will now come to order." Tower Falls' Judge Prudence Mayher stood tall and straight behind the podium.

"We're looking into the problem of Duck Lake."

"I make a motion that we close the lake until the source of the smell can be determined. "

"I second the motion. "

As growing discontent spread across the crowd, "You can't close the lake. My kids fish there and swim there!"

"Yeah and lately they are sick from doing that, there."

"Bull, they're sick from somethin goin around."

"Hold on! We need to discuss the problem. Miss Judge, this is supposed to be a civilized hearing."

"Any more outbursts like this and you'll be thrown out, Harley Davidson."

"Ain't fair, Miss Judge, ain't fair. My kids ain't the only ones sick."

"Sit down, Harley!"

"Miss Letty, I see you have your hand up."

"The problem with the lake, Your Honor, is the frog."

"Frog?"

"Yes, it drowned the man and spilled his beer. We need to go into imaginary time, which is real time, and save the man."

Judge Prudence Mayher coughed slightly covering her smile. "Are there any other proposals? Gentlemen! Harley, you're running your mouth again. Either say it out loud or keep quiet."

"Yes Ma'am, there's a bunch of us here wondering what imaginary time is."

Letty jumped to her feet and addressed the court. "Your Honor, if these silly men have read anything about Quantum Physics, they would know what I am talking about."

At this point, Oliver rose. "Your Honor, imaginary time aside, I move that we drag Duck Lake. Maybe even bring in some divers. Something is definitely causing some serious contamination to the lake. Dragging it would clear out any debris that could be causing the problem. "

Letty, still standing, seconded the motion.

"All those in favor?"

"We haven't even begun to discuss all that is involved with dragging the lake."

"Alright Harley, what needs to be discussed?"

160

"Who's going to do it and how much is it going to cost? We don't even know if it's the lake that's making our kids sick."

"I had the water tested," responded Oliver. "It's contaminated. Oh, I paid for it myself."

"Letty and I will pay all expenses for the lake. Mr. Harley doesn't have to worry about the town's budget, or donating any money to the project."

"Thank you Annie! All those in favor?" asked the judge. "Done! Mr. Homes, it's all up to you. Get what you need. Also see to it that you keep the court informed."

"Oh! Another woman boss," Oliver whispered to himself and he turned to leave.

Dickie opened the door and stepped inside. The large room was darkened, but at the far end a light lit the circular staircase leading up. A little uneasy, he walked to the stairs and hollered, "Katherine, are you here?" His question was met with silence, then, he heard a shuffling and a door open. He swallowed deep as she appeared at the top of the staircase with only a towel around her.

"Dickie!" Katherine flew down the stairs and threw her arms around him almost knocking him over. "It's you, it's really you. Let me look at you, touch you." Her towel fell to the floor revealing her slim body and long slender legs.

Dickie stepped back as the towel fell and immediately bent to pick it up. With the towel in front of him blocking his view, "Here Katherine, someone might see you— wrap up, please."

"Dickie, what's gotten into you? She wrapped the towel around herself and tucked it neatly. Her eyes narrowed. "Where have you been? What leggy 'babe' have you been with now?"

"It's a long story." He noticed the flower arrangement on a coffee table and a figure of a sleeping cat in bronze on the raised hearth. There were flames in the fireplace.

"A long story? I've been worried sick. The police and everyone else in town have been looking for you, and all you have to say for yourself is, 'It's a long story'?"

"Put some clothes on and we'll talk."

161

"Yeah, you bet we'll talk," she blurted out as she headed back up the stairs. "I'll be right back. You had better be here."

Miraculously she made a second entrance down the staircase in only a few minutes. Dickie had reclined on the sofa.

"Dickie! Dickie! Richard Bearzall!"

Through unfocused eyes, Dickie half-waved one arm weakly and let it fall. "War mongers. . . so much water. . . so much water."

Frowning, she leaned over him. "Dickie?"

"Murderers, pain, so much pain," he slurred.

"Oh, poor baby. You need to rest. We'll talk tomorrow." She swung his legs up on the sofa and pushed gently on his shoulder.

He fell face first into the pillow, then roused enough to say, "Oliver?"

Maybe I should call someone. Why was he asking for Oliver? I'll call Oliver, no, the doctor. It's too late to call anyone now. I'll make the calls in the morning. I hope I can stay awake. Look at him! Poor baby. I've missed you so much. She touched his face gently.

Early the next morning, Katherine woke with a start. Then she remembered. *Dickie's home. I have to make coffee. He likes his coffee.* Hurriedly, she pulled her robe tighter, took a deep breath and patted her cheeks before heading downstairs. She bent down over the back of the sofa and reached out to hug her long lost husband. The sofa was empty.

CHAPTER 17

The Good Bye Social

"As most of you have already heard, this is my last Sunday here. I will be leaving on sabbatical— " After a short pause, Father Paul broke the silence with, "I'm coming back in a few months. I will be speaking in various places in support of our program here for the deaf, so it won't all be for rest and relaxation. This is also a joyous occasion. Your interim priest is with us today. I would like to introduce Father Luke. After service there will be punch and refreshment in the fellowship hall. Please stay and welcome Father Luke."

Katherine dabbed her eyes with a dainty crocheted hanky. She had Jonah cornered by the punch and finger food table. "Jonah, I dreamed Dickie came home. What an emotional traumatic night. And now Father Paul is leaving. I really need him to stay."

"And this elaborate social is making it even more emotional. I'm sorry Katherine. I don't know what to do either." Jonah was quick to change the subject. "Who did the decorations?"

"Charity and a couple of other ladies from the church. Jonah, why haven't you come to see me— Dickie's best friend. I feel like you've deserted me. And Penn, he hasn't even called to see if I needed anything. Some friends you two turned out to be!"

"I'm still under suspicion Katherine. I don't want it to look like I'm seeing you. Penn, well that's another story, he'll be around here soon."

"Everyone has deserted me, I've never been so alone in my life."

"What can I do? You know I care. I don't want to put you under suspicion either."

"To hell with them all! I have to have my friends around me."

"You know life's lonely, no one knows that better than me."

"How is Annie?" Her sarcasm was not missed.

"Hey you guys!" Charity pushed her way toward them. "You can't monopolize this corner. Meet Father Luke."

"Father, I understand you're a fisherman."

"Why yes, I heard you like to fish as well."

"That I do. How about a get-together some time soon?"

"Charity, these two obviously have something in common. Lets go over here and let them talk fish." Her tone told Charity, Katherine needed to talk. "I was sure I was awake. It was so real. I even pinched myself." Her eyes welled up with tears as her voice trailed off.

"Hey! I know you miss him terribly, Katherine, maybe its an omen. He'll be back." Charity smiled and gave Katherine a hug.

"Maybe." She smiled weakly.

As Katherine approached Father Paul she told him, "we will miss you, Father, but of course we realize the importance of your work with the deaf children. Will you be needing any more financial assistance?"

"Katherine, you've already been more than generous. I have everything I need. The whole community has been more than generous."

"I'm at a loss for words. I was frightened out of my wits. I was sure someone was after me, so I hid out in the old cave. Please, please, Katherine, don't be angry with me." Dickie pleaded.

"Angry! I am more than angry. I thought you were dead. So did everyone else. I'm angry, happy, sad, confused, all of this because of you!" Katherine raised her voice, then whispered "I still love you."

"I know it was the wrong thing to do, but I was scared to death. I didn't mean to frighten you, or anyone, and I love you too. You know that, don't you?"

"I love you Richard Bearzall. I have loved you since we were in high school. Why do you think I married you? Still, it will take time to heal all the hurt and understand all the emotions. We will survive."

Dr. Boney entered the room, "Well you certainly took good care of yourself while 'hiding' out. All the tests have come back. Everything is fine, just perfect." He raised his eyebrows then added, "There's a detective here to talk to you two, says its important. Should I show him in?"

Dickey and Katherine both nodded.

"Hello Professor, Katherine, I have a few questions."

"Just a few? I'd think you would have more than a few!"

Dickie hung his head and plaintively begged "Katherine, please, don't be angry. I'm sorry."

"Would you two rather do this at the station or your home or here? I am open to options." Oliver waited a while for an answer, then "I guess its up to me. Lets head on down to the station."

"No! No, I would rather be home. We'll meet you there." Katherine tugged at Dickie's sleeve.

"I'll drive you home."

"I have my car. We'll meet you there."

"Maybe you misunderstood me, I'll drive you home. He is not going to disappear again, not on my watch." Oliver asserted his authority and ushered them out to his car.

"Yeah! No harm, no foul. I don't agree. He should be prosecuted for something! We spent the better part of the summer looking for him. We even had Duck Lake dragged, twice!" Madelynn fumed. "Don't you have something to do Oliver?"

"Yes maam. I am going over to the Bearzall's estate. They

are having a welcome home party for Dickie. You're invited too. You coming?'

"Absolutely not! I just told you how I feel. He needs to go to jail."

"He isn't talking anymore, maybe he really did witness the murder!" Katherine hugged herself and shivered.

"What murder?"

"You remember, over at Strafford, didn't you hear about the murder and theft that happened while we were there?"

"You mean during the Shakespearian Event?"

"Yes. We were there and Dickie says he saw it happen— "

"No wonder he's being so quiet. He might be in danger. He should go to Oliver, he would know what to do." Charity whispered.

"He won't."

"Annie, what are you doing? Why do you have the door locked?"

"Just a minute. There, hurry, don't let anyone see you come in here."

"What's going on? Who else is here?"

"Never mind. Look!"

"Tea leaves? Is that what that is in your cup?"

"Yes. Look at the picture in the bottom of the cup."

"It's a picture of Ali. What, how did you do that?"

"I didn't. It's the tea leaves. Look, there's an X under his face, just like a skull and cross-bones."

"What does that mean?"

"I don't know. Maybe he's poison."

"Maybe Ali isn't who he says he is. Maybe he's trying to hurt my precious. Oh, you don't suppose? Annie! There's someone prowling around. Annie, do you hear that? We'd better see who it is—no, I'm too frightened."

"Jonah! How did you get in the kitchen without us hearing you?"

"Through the door. You two were so engrossed in your conversation, you didn't notice. Anyone could get in."

166

"Would you like to join us for tea?" Letty reached for the tea pot, but Jonah didn't take his eyes off Annie.

"Maybe you'd better sit down. You look rather peeked. Are you alright?"

"I think so."

"I came up here to tell you Oliver thinks there may be more going on than we know about."

"You mean the Penn thing? Or Dickie thing? I thought that was all cleared up. Isn't everyone accounted for?"

"Well, yes, all the missing have been found. But Dickie insists he witnessed a murder down in Strafford. He is also sure it has something to do with the theft of the manuscript." Jonah shrugged and eyed Annie and Letty, waiting for any hint they might have some answers.

"He was murdered. I told you, the frog grabbed him and he didn't come back up." Letty was wide eyed as she looked from one to the other. A sense of realization began to creep in.

"Who was murdered?"

With a deep sigh Letty said "Bearzall! How many times do I have to tell you? The frogs got him!"

Annie and Jonah shook their heads.

"Jonah, Letty is not, um, right. You know that don't you?" She whispered.

He nodded in agreement.

"Letty—shush!" Turning back to Jonah, "You must have been the noises Letty and I heard a while ago. Why would you be sneaking in here like that?"

"Sneaking? I wasn't sneaking! Are you sure you ladies are okay?"

"Of course, do you think the boogie man's lurking in the shadows?"

"I didn't make any noises. I think I had better check out Planet Venus for you."

Jonah led the way and suddenly stopped short— **HOLY MOSES**!!!

Annie stood behind Jonah, peering around him, then with a gasp she grabbed for his arm. "It's Ali."

"It's okay, he's not going to hurt anyone anymore. Do you know where Oliver is, Annie? Letty, Annie's as white as a

167

ghost, I mean, a sheet. Annie, it's okay."

"What are we going to do?" Letty strained to see. "Oh no! Jonah, we didn't do this! Oh no, not again. How can this happen again?"

"Of course you didn't"

"Maybe he's after more than Jezebel. Do you remember how quick he denied being a diver?"

"That sure enough's a wet suit."

"Jonah, get Annie some Alke Seltzer. I'll call 911."

"Letty, before you call 911, do you know where Oliver is?"

"He and Barbie went out tonight. We have his beeper number."

"Leave him a message, then call 911."

"911, please help us, my precious Jezebel has murdered someone."

"Calm down Ma'am, where do you live?"

"This is Letty Tower at the Tower Estate."

"Don't hang up. We'll send someone right out. Keep talking. Who got murdered?"

"Ali Ases, I think. Jonah said Ali—"

"So, there's other people there too?"

"Yes, my sister and her— "

"Are any of you in danger?"

"I don't think so, Jezebel loves me. She wouldn't hurt Annie. Oh no, she tried to eat Jonah once."

"Stay calm, can you hear the sirens yet?"

"This is a well insulated house. You know, my Papa was prudent about that. My mother caught pneumonia easily—"

"Letty, can you hear the sirens?"

"Papa sent us upstairs when anything upsetting happened. I think I'll go upstairs now."

"Please Letty, don't hang up! Put Annie on the phone."

"Annie's ill. Jonah's getting her some Alke Seltzer."

"Put Jonah on the phone."

"Jonah, you're wanted on the phone."

"Tell them to call back later."

"Okay! He said he will call you back later."

At that moment, someone pounded loudly on the lion's head. Jonah looked toward Annie, "Are you expecting anyone?"

"No."

"Let me go to the door alone."

Annie and Letty reached for each other's hand.

"Are you scared, Sissy? Maybe they sent another frog."

"Yes, Letty, I'm scared."

"Oliver, come on in. I'm glad its you. I'll tell the ladies you are here."

"Jonah, some information came back we've been waiting for. Your 911 call came in at the same time. The man Jezebel ate was H.M. Kellamov. He's involved in at least four unsolved murders. The FBI has quite a file on him. This puts the sisters at risk. There was the theft of an old manuscript, then a murder down at Strafford, Dickie's murder. The one he said he saw, then his own murder. This is definitely bigger than we can even imagine."

"Whoa, isn't Dickie home? Boy Oliver, I thought I was confused."

"Jonah, you go find Penn and the other guy and meet me at the Branch. Quick as possible. Annie, Letty. Now where did they go?"

"I can only guess, but I heard Letty say something about hiding in the closet. Should I go get them?" *What does he mean "the other guy?" It's Dickie!* Jonah stared at Oliver, *this is too strange. I know what it is, he has been staying here with the ladies and has lost it too.*

"No. Let them hide. We'll know where they are when we need them."

CHAPTER 18

Guy's Night Out

Oliver had information he knew he had to share with the other men. "Glad you guys could meet me here. There are things you don't know," Oliver began.

"Things I don't know—I've been in the dark all my life—"

"Come on Jonah, Penn, and, uh, ah, what do we call you? We need to be serious for a minute. Let's move to the corner."

"I thought I was in the dark. We call him Dickie."

Oliver shot Dickie a quick glance, motioning the three to follow him.

Once in the corner they became so engrossed in their whispering, they didn't realize that three men from another table were trying to eavesdrop.

"Do you mean, all this time?" whispered Jonah.

"Keep your voice down. We have to keep this to ourselves."

"Yeah but, Katherine?"

"No— and its really difficult. I'm having a hard time with this." Dickie asserted.

Penn's weird sense of humor was shining through— "I'll just bet you are. All this time? I thought we were friends—"

"We are friends. Stop laughing."

"This has got to be the funniest thing I've ever heard."

"Cool it, you guys. It was my idea to keep it quiet," inserted Oliver.

171

"Do you really think you can pull this off?"

"We have so far."

The three men behind them moved closer. As they did so, they got into a friendly scuffle. Oliver noticed one of them had a dagger on his wrist when his watch band broke and fell to the floor.

The man locked eyes with Oliver and Oliver soon realized that he and his friends were in a great deal of danger. He must get the other three out of there. Pretending to be really tipsy, Oliver started for the dressing room behind the bar and down the hall. "Where's the long-legged dancer," he slurs. "I gotta find my sweetheart."

Penn, Dickie, and Jonah, all three follow after him, trying to keep him from going into the dressing room.

"Oliver, what's gotten into you? You can't go in there. It's the ladies' dressing room."

As Oliver reached the door, he turned to see three figures following close behind. "Get in here, quick! Don't look back, there's three guys hot on our trail, hurry!"

"What are you talking about?"

"Dickie, the guy sitting behind me has a dagger on his wrist, just like Ali's. Come on, let's get outta here."

"What are you talking about? How are we supposed to get out?"

The four men stood staring at one another as the pounding at the door increased. Hanging on the wall to one side, were costumes the dancers used.

"I'll be a singing maestro and entertain for a few minutes," said Oliver as he slipped on a jacket and top hat. "Hurry and get into something and promenade across stage. The back door is across the stage and to the left."

"You'd better know what you're talking about," said Dickie as Oliver bounced out on stage and began to sing. Soon the piano joined in and he sang the house down while the other three were desperately looking for costumes, and then, out they came. They pranced across the stage in long slinky dresses, furs, and hi-heels. Bearzall, as a well corseted blond, Penn as a leggy red headed belly dancer, and Jonah, as an over-sized full busted platinum floozy.

"Oh man, I like tall women. Come on baby, lay one on me,

right here."

The drunk was advancing toward them at a steady pace. "What do I do now, Penn? Come on friend, help me out." The three men had fans, waving them frantically as they pirouetted, dipped and strutted around. Penn and Bearzall were laughing so hard they could hardly keep the fans going.

"Plant one on him and exit, stage left, friend, and hurry up. Let's boogie."

"Come on, Jonalene, shake that booty and let's get out of here, and don't look back, go, now!"

"I'm going, I'm going."

"You got a car, little man?"

"Sure."

"Baby, you've just been invited. Gimme the keys please."

"The maestro's done— he's going too."

"Oh that's great. I've gotta share you ladies with another guy?"

"Life's full of cherry pits sometimes. We're outta here."

As the four left with their new-found friend, they pushed the dumpster up against the back door and all piled into a brand new gold Caddy.

"Where's the keys, little man?" Penn was getting impatient.

"Hey, you're not a woman!"

"Nobody's perfect. Hit it Penn, we're outta here."

"Here they come. Count them Dickie. How many are there?"

"I count three, no—wait a minute. Ali Ases is with them, I'll be darned."

"Where do we go from here Oliver?"

"You aaaaa, ladies are in a real jam, huh? It looks like you need help. Wanna come spend the night at my place? I have security."

"Sounds good to me. What about you Jonah?"

"Do we have any other options?"

"We'll discuss options later."

"No one will get to you at my place. I can guarantee you that. What is this anyway, someone got an irate husband?"

"Something like that."

When they got to the little guy's place, security let them in

173

and he led the way in through an enormous foyer into an eighteenth Century sitting parlor done in Lebanese Cedar and royal purple. Ivory statuettes from Africa lined the giant mantle. The trophy heads of successful safaries joined generations of family portraits, hung high on the tapestried walls.

"Make yerselves ta home, ladies, while I get ta know this ravishing platinum Amazon," he slurs as he pats Jonah's behind.

"Watch it, buster,, I'm not drunk enough for that yet."

"Voula! The little man pressed the secret button and a full-wall bar emerged, stocked with the world's best. "Drink ta yer heart's content, I don't drink alone."

"None of us do, little guy. If you want us to drink, you have to drink with us."

"Don't mind if I do," he slurred. "Let me show ya my favorite drink."

"What's that?"

"Black Russian. It'll knock yer pantyhose off."

Jonah giggled, "okay, little man, bring it on. Do you come with the drink?"

"Ya better believe it!"

"Hey Jonah, what's going on over there anyway? Did your party pal poop out on ya?"

"Gosh, he must have, he's on the floor. That musta been a big man's drink. I'll let him have mine too. How do we get outta here?"

"There's too many dogs to run for it. Any ideas, Dickie?"

"You guys ever watch Tarzan?"

"AaaAaaAaaaaaaa—"

"Hey, this guy's a natural. We've got a ready-made Tarzan here. Now, if we're going to fly through trees, we're going to have to ditch these clothes."

"Not so fast. I kinda like this, the girdle and the pantyhose might come in handy, besides, did any of you think to bring your own clothes along?"

"Ahhhh . . . guys, we've got a cross-dresser here. Hey Platnum Amazon, do you carry your own make-up with you too?"

"Cut the sarcasm, Penn, we need a real answer, quick! It's time to cut the hanky-panky and get out of here. The ladies may be in real trouble about now."

"About now? I thought that's what started this whole thing."

"Okay, so now how do we get outta here guys?"

"Dunno, maybe Penn has some brilliant ideas."

"Don't look at me. My brain goes to bed at ten."

"Oh, I see. Cinder fellow without his fairy godmother. "

"I think we ought to be getting back to the estate without any further delay. Oliver, you're the brains here, what's our next step?"

Detective Oliver and his three helpers, dressed for a faerie adventure climbed from an upstairs balcony to an outstretched Maple limb and preciously scooted, straddling the limb.

"Watch your crotch, guys, this could be dangerous."

"I knew this girdle was good for something. okay, Who's behind me? Back off, will ya?" Jonah was getting pretty uptight with Penn right behind him.

"What's the matter, pal?"

"The dogs below are getting closer to us."

"No, we're getting closer to them, hey Dickie, back off, you're too close. Watch out!"

Dickie lost his grip and slipped, taking a head-long dive—until he was caught by his corset. There he hung, up-side-down from the over-burdened limb. Hanging mid-air, knees bent, he solemnly and deliberately crossed himself. The picture couldn't have been more perfect, only it was all up-side-down. There he was, his hands folded, his knees bent, kneeling in prayer.

"Father in Heaven, I really try to be good, mostly I don't make it—but I do try, honestly . . . as You can see, I really need Your help right now, please! Right now, Father, please!"

Seconds later, the big barking dogs turned their attentions to the front of the big house, and then ran for the front gate. The four adventurers dropped to the ground and ran for the back wall. Well, not quite four—

"Hey guys, help me down!"

"Penn, we're forgetting something!"

175

"What's that?"

"Dickie!"

"At least he doesn't have to worry about the little guy. He likes ravishing platinum amazons."

"Ya ya, rub it in, you're never going to let me live this one down, are you? If you ever tell Annie, I'll strangle you!"

"Come on, help me with Dickie's corset."

"You know, I just thought of something."

"What's that?"

"How are we going to get to the Estate dressed like this?

"The only way to the Estate is through town. To our places as well, what now?"

"We're not far from a friend's house," ventured Oliver.

"What kind of a friend is this?"

"Well, a good friend . . . my girl friend."

"Oliver, you sly fox, you. Is this someone we know?"

"Probably."

"Who? Do you have any clothes there? Come on, Oliver, it's time to fess up."

"Well, maybe, in a pinch you understand. I keep a couple of changes of clothes there just in case— "

"Oliver, you're a lifesaver. This couldn't have worked out better if we'd planned it. Dickie and I can wear your clothes, in a pinch, but,what about— ?"

"Yeah, what am I going to wear?"

"I thought you liked your pantyhose and pink boa."

"It's not far from here. Just down around that corner."

"Wait up guys. I can't run in heels."

"Take'm off good buddy."

"On this gravel?"

"I just twisted my ankle, come on guys."

"Do you want the bad guys to catch up with us?"

"My ankle's fine— really."

"Then do you suppose you could move a little faster?"

As the four reached Barbie's house, Oliver pounded on the door, "Barbie, are you home?"

"What's the matter, don'tcha have a key?"

"Of course I do, but maybe she's home."

Barbie came to the door. "What's going on? Oliver, is that you? Who are your friends?"

"Barbie, we don't have time for this— this is business. The bad guys are right behind us. Let us in, please!"

As Barbie opened the door wider, a look of amusement swept across her face.

Forgive me, but I have to ask, are the bad guys horny? It's not every night I see six-foot ladies of the night being chased through the street by bad guys."

"Barbie, hurry, let us in. You haven't put my clothes in the washer yet. Tell me you haven't?"

"In the washer and dryer and folded. What's going on?"

"We need them desperately!"

"I can see that. Stay right here. I'm going to get my camera."

"Don't you dare. Let us in!"

"Come on in."

As they charge through the door Barbie flashed, twice.

"I can't see."

"That's alright. You never could, remember? You're always in the dark."

"That outfit looks just about as silly on you as the fancy gown, Penn."

"Just call me Bozo." Penn spun around showing off how Oliver's oversized clothing fit. "Anyway, Oliver, who are those guys and why are they so hot to get us?"

Oliver took a small piece of paper out of his pocket and showed it to them.

"Look't this! That symbol was on the threatening letters." Dickie was shaking. "What does this mean, Oliver?"

"What threatening letters, would someone tell me what's going on here," asked Jonah?

"This little dagger is some sort of mob identifier. Ali had one on his wrist under his watch, and so did the guys sitting behind us at the Buzzard's Branch. I saw his when his watchband broke."

They charged into the night again. When they reached the Estate, Letty was overjoyed and alone.

"Letty, are you alright? Where's Annie?"

"Penn, I'm so glad to see you. Where have you been?"

"I'm okay. Where's Annie?"

"I don't know. Why are you interested in Annie? Is that you Jonah? How cute! Does Annie know?"

"Letty, this is important. Where's Annie?"

"She hasn't come back and it's really late."

"Letty, why did she leave? I thought you two were hiding. Are there bicycles or anything with wheels around here?"

"There's an Indian in the garage. Why?"

"We ran out of gas."

"Did I ever tell you?"

"Not now! Do you have anything with wheels?"

"I told you, there is an Indian in the garage."

"No, we're not going on the warpath. A bicycle or anything with wheels, you know?" Jonah couldn't help but smile.

"Yes, the Indian has a side-car and the key's in the switch. I don't know whether it still runs or not. But Harold keeps all our machines running, I think"

"Are you talking about a motorcycle," asked Oliver? "My dad had one of those, a big Indian."

"Yes that's the one. Let me see, it's a— what was that shift? It is a something about killing-yourself-shift."

"A suicide shift," said Oliver. "I think I can handle it. Come on Jonah."

"I'm in the dark again. Where are we going now?"

"We're going to look for Annie. Letty, do you have any idea where she was going when she left here?"

"She was going to pick up some groceries, but that was three hours ago. Maybe, let me think. She was talking about that new café at the bookstore."

Oliver dashed for the phone. "Bunnie, put your ears on, please! Damn, where are my ears. Bunnie! Come in, come in!"

"Oliver, is that you? This isn't a radio, Oliver. Boy is the Hatter mad. Where are you?"

"Bunnie, listen. Annie's disappeared. This is an emergency. We need help. Call Centerville and get back-up. Do not call Madelynn for any reason. Not till I tell you to, understand?"

"Yes, Olie, I think I do."

"Penn, you and Dickie wait here with Letty and help her pack. I can't wait for back-up. I'm headed for Cashe's Market. When help arrives, send them in that direction. When I get there, I'll call you."

They sped off through the night, Oliver in command of the big motor-cycle and Jonah, in the side car, still in full dress, his long pink silk scarf flapping in the breeze.

CHAPTER 19

The Indian

The man leaned over the counter and whispered to Annie, "I think you're being followed."

"What?"

"Don't look now, but I think the man who just came in has been watching you. From outside. You in some sort of trouble?"

"I could be. Is there a back exit? Do you have a back door?"

"The back door's over there," he whispered. "I'll keep him busy while you leave. Be careful, there aren't any lights in the alley. Turn left and don't stop. Head for the light at the end of the alley. Scream if you need help. I'll call the police too."

"Thank you." Annie burst through the door. She turned, running. Her heart was pounding. She could hardly catch her breath. She could see the light ahead as her feet were crying out, "Please don't let me stumble, please— just a few more steps, please."

A deafening roar overtook her. She was swept off her feet. She was tightly constricted by her captor's arms. "You brute! Let me go! She kicked, trying desperately to free herself. She twisted but was jerked down, her head snapped back, "Oliver! Thank God! I'm so glad it's you! You scared me half to death! I can't get my breath—" Then she spied Jonah. As she regained her breath, a smile crossed her face. "Jonah? What are you . . . ?"

"Not now! I'll explain later."

"Welcome aboard! Hang on tight!" Oliver shouted.

The trio roared off into the night.

"Oliver you missed the turn!" Jonah howled at the top of his voice.

"No I didn't. That car cut us off. We'll have to make a run for it this way."

"This is a dead end! Oliver! Turn around!"

"Not so! I know where I'm going. I just hope that rickety old bridge will hold up!" Oliver yelled back.

Annie was white with fear, eyes bulging, mouth moving but no sound would come out.

"Jonah? Is Annie alright?"

"She seems to be."

"Duck! Branches! Hold on! Here we go!" The big Indian made a quick turn to the right. Bang! Bang! Clatter! Bang! The boards rattled thunderously, the Indian shook violently, Oliver, Annie and Jonah wailed. The Indian tipped as Oliver made another sharp turn. *Oh crap we're going to tip over! Please not now!*

Jonah thrust himself out over the side, he braced his feet under the seat. "Maybe this will keep us upright!"

Annie lashed out wildly. She grabbed at Jonah. "What are you doing?" She caught hold of him. She jerked him back into the sidecar.

"Wow! That was close! Jonah, can you pilot this thing?" Oliver's voice was cracking as he tried to shout over the roar of the Indian and the screams of Annie and Jonah.

Jonah wildly grabbed at his pink scarf, sputtering and gasping for air. He shook his head, gulped and finally got the knot untied. A weak "No" was all he could manage.

"Sorry Jonah. I didn't mean to choke you." Annie stood up, leaned out and straddled the seat. "I can."

"Slow down just enough so I can jump off. I have to get to the station! You two head for Bearzall's!"

"I'll take you there. I know a shortcut!" Annie yelled as she accelerated off the road. Down through the golf course they went.

"Crap! There is another bridge up above this one. They've crossed it, too." Goonie panted.

"Never mind. Come on! We need to get the loot and get the heck out of here. Now!" A husky voice rasped. "Get this damn thing turned around." She knew the chase was over. She also knew Oliver had put everything together and she had to disappear, fast! "No screw ups now or we're toast!"

The Special Unit and the Swat Teams from Centerville and Oliver all shouted "freeze!" when Hattie Kellamov, Mills Kellamov, and Snitch Goonie sprinted out the back door. "We've been waiting for you." Oliver's absolute joy could not be missed. Neither could the look of total surprise.

The blinding lights pasted a picture perfect shadow of the three; three statues with arms raised, in mid stride, frozen in place.

"Gotcha!" Oliver nodded his head. "Cuff 'em. Read 'em their rights. Book 'em."

"I wanted you all here so I can put this mess to rest. I'll try to be brief. So if you have questions, please wait till I'm done." Oliver stated with authority. He was quite pleased with himself as he began to relate how he put "two and two" together.

"I'd gotten a fax from the Centerville Police, they had found the identity of their 'John Doe'. I asked for and they sent me his name and picture. He had been identified as Louie Kellamov, a mobster. I realized Ali Ases and Madelynn looked very similar. Penn and Dickie had disappeared. I came up here and Harold told me about the satchel Ulga found. I checked it out. It had the stolen manuscript in it. I knew Annie and Letty didn't steal it. So I had to come up with a plan."

"In the meantime I'd found the old wooden bridge and unfortunately stumbled across Dickie's body," Oliver paused putting his hand up, "no questions now. I had the terrible task of telling Katherine. At that time I confided in her my suspicions and she knew some surprising facts and offered to help. Her biggest surprise; Dickie and Father Paul were identical twins. I went to Father Paul and he said he would 'go on a sabbatical' and take Dickie's place. He prayed for our success. Not now Letty. I called Centerville, they agreed to Katherine's, Father Paul's and my plan.

"Annie and Letty wanted to take me to England. I was worried Madelynn would take off, but remembered she had some unfinished business to take care of. Centerville police said they would keep their eyes on the mob for me. When we got back, we put the plan into action.

"Harold called Madelynn, he told her about the satchel and she had Snitch Goonie pick it up. She had called him Officer Thivee, and told Harold not to discuss the satchel or the exchange with anyone. He promised he wouldn't. She took our bait. Our next step was to wait for them to make a move. It was a terrible waiting game! By the way, Father Luke is really Mills Kellamov. Real cleaver, that one." He took a deep breath and let it out slowly.

"Now you all remember Dickie said he'd seen a murder? He had. He had also inadvertently taken a picture of it. He gave his film to Penn, for safe keeping and as we all know, Penn hid it in a little black box, in his pickup. We also know what happened to his pickup." He stopped and cleared his throat. "But what some of you don't know, Letty, with the help of Annie," he paused again eyeing Annie, "had stolen the little black box from the recovered pickup. Letty hid it, along with her teddy bear, Mr. Teddy. The film is really important. It shows who murdered Louie Kellamov, it might also contain a picture of the others who are involved. So, that leaves us with finding Mr. Teddy, which leads us to Letty." Oliver turned to the chair, palms up, "Where's Letty? Where's Annie? Oh, no! They've gone and hid again." He bit his lower lip.

"No Oliver, I've not gone into hiding." Annie was beaming. "Letty said she 'stuffed' Mr. Teddy like she had Penn. I found him in her big closet, she hid him under the floor boards. He has something hard in him. Here, you look." Annie handed the teddy over to Oliver.

Oliver carefully opened Mr. Teddy's back. The Centerville police, the Special Unit and Swat Teams all moved in closer for a good look. There it was! The missing black box and inside, the film. "Now we have more proof to put the Kellamov mob away for a long, long time!" Oliver broke out into a huge grin. "Did I leave anything out?"

"Sorry, Oliver," Centerville's Chief grimaced "you have them on the satchel, sort of. They were caught with it, yes. They say there was a quick buck to be made, at the expense of Annie and Letty. They still point the finger for the theft at Annie and Letty. And sorry to say, the ladies did have it first." He shrugged.

Oliver laughed. "Well they could, but Snitch put it in the wrong motel room, he confessed to that. He also put something else in it." He was feeling quite smug, then continued, "Snitch thought they were all leaving the country. He put their passports in the satchel too. So, we got em good!"

The group gathered together all nodded in agreement and let out a sigh.

Letty entered the parlor, tray rattling, smiling broadly ask, "Lemonade anyone?"

They all shuddered.

Epilogue

Hattie Kellamov and her brother Mills Kellamov are spending the rest of their lives in a federal penitentiary. Life without possibility of parole.

Snitch Goonie is serving his sentence of thirty years in a federal correctional facility. He will be up for parole in ten, for cooperating with authorities.

Bunnie Mann is Tower Falls' first female detective.

Harold Hoehandler and Ulga Dustoffer married. The Tower "Girls" bought the newly weds Penny O'Coins' house for a wedding present. They both still work for the "Girls".

Father Paul is back from his sabbatical. He acquired many sponsors and was able to hire three new teachers for the orphanage.

Penny O'Coins and Katherine Bearzall dated for awhile before they eloped to Reno. They live in the Bearzall's Estate.

Jonah Souser and Annie Tower go on photography trips quite often. They are "just friends."

Oliver S. Homes has been officially adopted by Annie Tower and Letty Tower. He and Barbie Toy are engaged. No date has been set. He is Chief Detective of the Tower Falls Police.

Letty Tower, that's another story.

The End

About the Author
(Authors)

Sheryl Hamilton Chaney and Netty Harris both live in southwestern Oregon. They were returning college students when they met and formed a lasting friendship as they completed their degrees. Sheryl Chaney and Netty Harris write under the pen name of Oliver Tower.

The idea for this book sprang from incidents Netty saw at a Shakespearian Festival. Both like attending each year.

Sheryl Chaney is also the author of *SandPrints A Collection of Poetry and Prose*, also available from Brilliant Book Press.

She's also launching a business with her daughter Karen Sterling that sells "Go For the Gold Rose Hip Tea," made from rose hips hand picked in the wilderness in Oregon. This healthy tea is full of Vitamin C and embodies the wild scent of Oregon itself!

Visit her website at www.beachpoet.com to read more about her, her writing and her tea business.

The love for both writing and business run in the family. Sheryl's other daughter owns Brilliant Book Press and its imprint Bravado Publishing.

To contact the authors of this book, email comments@kristen-bailey.com or visit www.beachpoet.com.

Sandprints A Collection of Poetry
and Prose

Sheryl Hamilton Chaney

Sandprints A Collection of Poetry and Prose
by Sheryl Hamilton Chaney
www.beachpoet.com

"Ashes and Mist"

My words fall as ashes
No one hears
Such a small thing—
To make no shadow.

My tears become mist
As a vapor
Rising in despair—
And are no more.

My song becomes silent
Passed as a cloud
I look and I see—
And my heart follows my eyes.

Sheryl Hamilton Chaney

The River People
by Kristen N. Bailey

Before fur traders or missionaries touched the Pacific Northwest... The River People flourished.

River Song lives in a valley of meandering streams that give them salmon to eat each spring. Oak trees abound in the valley. A forest of cedar and fir surround them, making a canopy and giving them planks for their longhouses, canoes, and totem poles. River Song's father, Chief Sits and Thinks, is growing old and sick. He trusts in her to lead their people. She must use her gift of words, especially when a wandering band of braves seeks a new home with them. Can this young girl hold her tribe together?

"A nicely told tale that discusses American Indians from a different perspective. It combines history with romance, with a hint of early women's liberation and a larger dose of Indian culture." *The Herald and News*

www.kristen-bailey.com   comments@kristen-bailey.com

Writing is a family tradition! Kristen Bailey is Sheryl Chaney's daughter and published their books through her own company. See www.bravadopublishing.com for more information on her writing, editing and publishing services, or email kristen@bravadopublishing.com.

www.ingramcontent.com/pod-product-compliance
Lightning Source LLC
Chambersburg PA
CBHW020607250626
47154CB00004B/1406